MR. FEBRUARY

Calendar Boys Series

NICOLE S. GOODIN

Mr. February
Published by Nicole S. Goodin
ISBN: 978-0-9951168-3-2
Copyright 2019 by Nicole S. Goodin
All rights reserved. ©
First published February 2019

Cover design by Nicole Goodin
Images purchased from Deposit Photos
Editing by Spell Bound

For all the babes born in February

CHAPTER ONE

Jackson

I toss back another shot even though I know it's a fucking terrible idea.

Everything has a blur to it and I know that as soon as I lie down, the whole god damn place is going to spin like crazy.

I poke at the bar with my finger, hopeful that it's somehow got less solid wood feeling in the past hour so that I might just be able to crash here rather than dragging my ass upstairs to bed.

I glance around the bar, lit only by a couple of dim lights now.

I feel sick – like about-to-chunder type of sick.

I know I *shouldn't* throw up in here—sending home all the staff so that I could go on a drinking bender means that if I vomit, I'll have to clean it up. No one is going to swoop in and save the day with a mop and bucket.

I'm all alone.

I might always be alone.

I reach for the bottle of bourbon, but the damn thing is empty.

"Stupid bourbon," I slur as I nudge the bottle away with my hand.

I contemplate going behind the bar and finding another bottle of something even stronger, but that would require moving, and I'm not particularly well equipped for moving right now.

"Oh *shit*. Where did everyone go?"

The female voice behind me should startle me, but I guess I'm way too drunk to be taken by surprise.

"Holy crap, how long have I been in the bathroom?"

"Sweetie," I slur as I spin around incredibly unsteady on the bar stool. "Don't ask me... I don't even know what day it is."

It takes a minute for the room to stop swaying, but when it does, my eyes land on a woman in a bright red dress.

Now, I might be drunk as fuck, but I'm still with it enough to know this chick is *hot*.

Not my usual type, but right now I need a blonde-haired, blue-eyed woman about as much as I need a hole in the head.

"*Damn*. You look smokin'," I drawl.

"And you look wasted," she replies with a grin and a shake of her head.

I try to lean back against the bar, in a cool, relaxed, non-drunk fashion and fail spectacularly, only just managing to somehow stay on the stool and avoid hitting the ground.

She walks closer and I can hear the click of her heels against the wood flooring.

"Well, *drunk guy*, it's been thrilling talking to you, but would you mind telling me how I get out of here?"

"*Can't*." I smirk. "We're shut. You're stuck in here forever. With me."

She laughs at my pathetic attempt at picking her up.

"Nice try, dreamboat, are you planning on sleeping on that stool tonight?"

I point upwards and nearly fall off my seat again.

"*Jesus,*" she says as she reaches out to help steady me.

"I live upstairs," I slur.

"Oh lord, you'll be lucky to make it two steps without tripping over your own feet with the state you're in."

She's so close to me now, she's holding onto my arm like I'm a baby who needs the help to sit up.

I grin up at her. She's really pretty and she smells so good. "You're *hot.*"

She shakes her head at me and laughs. "And surprisingly enough, you're still drunk."

"Ain't that the truth," I drawl.

"Drowning your sorrows?"

"How'd you know?"

"People don't usually celebrate alone, so..."

I blink my eyes together hard a few times. Everything is getting even blurrier.

"I need bed," I announce as I try to get to my feet.

"Truer words have never been spoken," she mumbles as she tries her best to help me stand.

"Go out the front," I tell her as the room *really* starts to spin. "Locks... on... its... own."

I take a step and it doesn't go well; the ground feels like it's trying to suck me in. I wonder if maybe I should let it.

"I'll be gine." I chuckle at myself. "I started to say good and then changed to fine."

"Oh, for the love of God," she mutters. "C'mon, I'll help you get upstairs."

"Knew you couldn't resist tryna get me into bed." I try to wink at her, but I don't think it works.

"Oh yeah, you're *totally* irresistible right now," she says as she drapes my arm over her shoulders and supports far more of my weight than she should. "Where are we heading, dreamboat?"

I point at the staircase on the far side of the room, and she huffs out a breath.

"Of course we are."

I open and shut my mouth a few times. My tongue feels fuzzy.

"Lizzie..."

"Katie," she corrects me as we amble across the room.

"No, no, Lizzie," I ramble.

"*Katie*," she repeats. "My name is Katie."

"No, Lizzie," I say again. "Not even a little bit."

I bury my face in her dark curly hair and breathe in deeply.

That's the last thing I remember.

CHAPTER TWO

Katie

"Hey, Tillie, it's me," I say in a hushed voice.

"Katie, where the fuck are you, girl? We lost you at the bar."

I can hear a club in the background. It's only early in Tillie's world. She'll be out for hours yet, hunting for eligible bachelors.

"I'm still at the bar."

"Did you meet a guy?" she asks excitedly.

"Not in the way you'd like to imagine." I roll my eyes as I glance at the very drunk male sprawled out across his bed. "I got stuck on the phone with Juliet and when I came out the whole place was shut down. There was just this wasted dude left drinking at the bar."

I can almost hear her eyes rolling through the phone. "So, let me guess, you're taking care of him?"

"*Maybe.*"

"You and your morals." She sighs. "Give him a bucket and come meet us for a dance," she pleads.

We both know she's wasting her breath. I won't be going anywhere until morning.

My silence is enough of an answer for her.

She sighs. "Send me a snap of him so I'll have something to show the police if he wakes up and murders you."

He's so drunk right now I know he couldn't hurt a fly even if he wanted to, but I do her one better and send her a picture of the driver's license I pulled out of his pocket before putting him to bed.

The drunk dreamboat has a name. And a hot name at that. *Jackson Matthews*.

"Done," I announce with a tap of my screen.

"Night, girl. Have fun on puke duty."

"Text me when you get home," I say.

"Will do." She giggles before the line goes dead.

He lets out a loud snore from the bed, and I shake my head in amusement.

I wander around the room looking at his stuff. I know it's rude but given I'm likely to deal with his spew some time during the next few hours, I figure a snoop is the least of what I'm owed.

He's got a whole stack of empty frames on one of his dressers, and dirty clothes and crap scattered all over the floor.

If I wasn't convinced he was single before, I would be now. He might have called me Lizzie about half a dozen times, but it's pretty clear there hasn't been a woman in this room for quite some time – if ever.

I find the bathroom down the hall and clean the makeup off my face and strip the tight, red dress from my body.

It feels weird to walk into his room in my underwear, but I know damn well that he's not going to be conscious for a long, long while.

I rummage around in his drawers until I find a t-shirt that will do for a nightie and slip it over my head.

I climb in the bed and do my best to shove him over enough so I have space to lie down.

There's no way I'm going to be able to get him under the covers, so I grab the rug off the end of the bed and drape it over him instead.

I've got a towel and a bucket set up right next to the bed, and if he doesn't need it at some point, I'll be shocked. The guy is totally wasted.

I check again that he's still lying on his side in a safe position before flicking off the light and closing my eyes.

***

I wake to the sound of retching and the stench of vomit. I groan and feel around for the light switch on the wall above my head.

I blink against the bright light and look over to see that he's getting most of it in the bucket.

I hop out of bed and pad down the hall to where I saw the kitchen earlier.

I fill up two glasses of water and rummage around in the cupboards and drawers until I find some pain killers – he's going to need them in the morning.

By the time I get back to the bedroom, he's passed out again, *and* on his back, so I roll him onto his side and take away the bucket of stink and the dirty towel.

I can't believe I'm cleaning up a stranger's vomit, but I know damn well that I won't be getting any more sleep if I don't do something about this smell. Plus, he's a super-hot stranger, so somehow, I manage to convince myself that it's not so bad.

I flush it down the toilet and rinse the bucket. I grab another clean towel and set everything back up again in case he decides he needs to go another round.

I take a sip of my own water after I climb back into his bed. I might not be anywhere near as drunk as he is, but I had the better part of a bottle of wine with dinner, plus the cocktails at the bar after, so I might be needing some of those pain killers myself if morning ever comes.

He groans in his sleep and I can feel him reaching around under the covers.

His hand finds my bare leg and rubs it slowly up and down.

I should push it away, I know I should, but I kind of like it. It's big and warm and gentle.

I close my eyes again as his hand stills on my leg and let sleep take me.

CHAPTER THREE

Jackson

I creep out of the bathroom as quietly as I can and wince at the sight of the mess in front of me.

There's shit *everywhere*, and this poor woman, whoever the hell she is, has likely seen it all – I've literally aired all my dirty laundry.

I try to kick a path clear as I make my way back to the bed.

I look in the bucket, expecting to find it full of spew, and I'm shocked to see that it's empty and clean.

I *definitely* puked last night. The stench coming from my breath when I woke up assured me of that.

I study the woman who is breathing lightly in her sleep.

She's wearing one of my t-shirts and her red dress is thrown over the chair in the corner, her heels and other girly crap are there too.

I feel like a total ass. I don't have the faintest idea who she is, let alone if anything happened between us last night.

I hope like hell I didn't fuck her – she's stunning and obviously kind hearted if she has in fact emptied my spew bucket – I'd hate to think that I touched her when I was barely conscious.

If you're going to be inside a woman that looks like that, you want to be able to remember it.

I sit down on the edge of the bed and chuckle quietly at the glass of water and the pain killers that are waiting on the bedside table for me.

I pop a couple and swallow them down gratefully. I got myself into one hell of a state last night if my pounding head and memory blanks are any indication.

I wrack my brain, trying to think what the fuck happened last night. I remember being alone – we closed up and I sent everyone home, so I can't figure out how this dark-haired goddess has found her way into my bed.

I recall a flash of the room spinning and someone calling me 'dreamboat', but I can't fill in the blanks... and there's a hell of a lot of them.

I've *really* got to stop fucking drinking like this.

I lie back down and roll over so I'm facing the stranger in my bed.

I run my finger over her cheek and she moves a little in her sleep.

She's beautiful.

"*Hey*... wake up," I say. *Jesus*. I don't even know her name. I'm a god damn embarrassment.

I rub my hand up and down her shoulder and arm and watch as her eyes start to sleepily open and shut.

Finally, they open all the way and focus on my face.

She's got the darkest brown eyes. They're so close to black, I've never seen anything like it.

"Good morning, Jackson Matthews," she says with a yawn.

I stare at her sheepishly and she giggles. "Katie," she prompts.

"*Katie*," I repeat, and it seems vaguely familiar to me.

"How's the head?" she asks.

"It's been better."

"I bet it has."

She doesn't seem embarrassed, or eager to escape, and I can't figure any of this out.

We stare at one another in silence before I remember I own a pair of balls and that it's about time I used them to figure out the sad state of affairs that is my life.

"I'm a little vague on the details of last night..." I say, embarrassment colouring my voice.

"That's not surprising..." she replies coyly.

"Did we..." I clear my throat awkwardly. "Did we... ah... did we have sex?"

She laughs and shakes her head. "No, Casanova, we did *not*."

Thank fuck for that.

"Did I kiss you?" I wince.

"Nope."

"I don't mean to sound like a prick... but what exactly are you doing here then?"

This is a new low for me. I'm mortified with myself right now.

She doesn't seem to mind though, in fact she laughs lightly.

"You were drunk. I helped you upstairs and put you to bed. I couldn't leave you here in the state you were in."

I close my eyes and take a deep breath. I'm seriously ashamed. "I vomited, didn't I?"

She nods solemnly. "Did you have pasta for dinner by any chance?"

I can feel my cheeks heating now. She giggles again in response to my obvious embarrassment.

I appreciate her help, I really do, but it's not right. She's a beautiful woman, and not all men have the same set of morals I do. She could have got herself into serious trouble coming into a stranger's bed like this.

I know people have one-night stands all the time, and I guess this might not be a new thing for her, but it still doesn't feel right.

"Why did you do this for me? I could have been a total psycho, and you just came up to my place."

She shrugs. "You seem harmless enough. And I just *couldn't* leave you like that."

I look at her in question. There's more to it than that. I can hear it in her tone.

She shudders. "My brother choked on his own vomit after a drinking session once. He would have died if his girlfriend wasn't with him that night to clear his airway and call an ambulance... I just couldn't risk you being another one of those statistics."

I don't know why, but my arms have goosebumps. This girl is seriously genuine, and I like that – even if she's taking risks with her own safety that she shouldn't.

"So..." She shrugs. "Are you going to tell me why you were down there drowning your sorrows?"

I wince again. I have no idea how much or how little I've told this woman but given that she's emptied out a bucket filled with my spew, I figure I owe her the truth at least.

"My fiancé. *Ex*-fiancé actually... she told me last week that she'd been cheating on me... with a mate of mine."

She grimaces. "Oh ouch. That's low."

"Yup."

"That level of drunk was probably quite justified then."

"I clearly thought so," I drawl.

"So, you still love her?"

That's not what I was expecting her to ask, but it would seem that Katie isn't like any of the women I'm used to meeting.

"I can't seem to turn it off," I admit.

"So, you're all over then?"

"She left me for him."

She nods. "Explains the empty frames. That really sucks."

I probably should care that she's seen all that, but surprisingly I don't. I feel comfortable around Katie... like I could tell her anything.

"You're preaching to the choir."

"Is her name Lizzie by any chance?" Katie asks me with her brow raised.

I groan. "How much did I say last night?"

"Not much. You called me Lizzie a couple of times..."

I frown at her. I don't know how drunk I would have had to be to call her Lizzie. They're *nothing* alike. I must have been well and truly on my own planet last night.

Lizzie is pale, blonde, stick-thin, and has light blue eyes.

Katie is olive-skinned, dark-haired, curvy, and has eyes like the night.

They couldn't be more different.

"Yup... that's my ex. She looks nothing like you... fuck, I'm really sorry if I called you that, her name is basically Satan at this point, so sorry for the insult."

She smiles at me. It lights up her whole face and causes deep dimples in both her cheeks. "Don't sweat it. And for the record, she sounds like an idiot."

"She is. Giving up all of this." I gesture to myself and she giggles softly.

I might not know anything much about Katie, but I like her. This chick is seriously cool. I haven't talked like this – this real – with someone in a long time.

She's looking at me as though she can feel it too – this connection between us.

"Thank you for looking out for me," I murmur as I watch her lips rubbing together.

"It's really not a problem," she whispers back.

I can feel this tension building in the air that I can't explain. We're strangers. It shouldn't feel like this.

"I didn't touch you last night, did I?" I ask as I inch a little closer to her.

"Your hand rubbed my leg," she says as she moves nearer too.

"Just your leg?"

"Just my leg," she whispers.

We're close now, so close that I could just lean forward and kiss her if I wanted to.

It shocks me that I *do* want to.

Bryn took me out right after Lizzie broke up with me and told me to screw her out of my system, but I couldn't do it. I couldn't even look at another woman, let alone fuck one.

But I'm looking at Katie now. And I like what I'm seeing. I like it a whole lot.

She's *nothing* like Lizzie. She's exactly what I need right now.

I reach out under the covers and find her thigh.

I don't know what I did last night, but I touch her how I imagine I would have.

Her dark eyes haven't left mine as I run my fingers up and down her leg.

"Like that?" I ask.

"Higher," she whispers.

I follow her request and go higher.

I can feel the hem of my t-shirt and if I go much higher, I'll find her underwear – if she's wearing any that is.

The thought of her bare in my sheets gets me hard in an instant. I didn't think I'd want a woman in this way for a long time, but damn, I don't just want her. I *need* her. I need her bad.

"If you don't want me - *this*, you better say something, Katie. Right now. Because fuck I want you."

She doesn't say a word. Her only response is to slide her hand down my arm and urge my hand higher until I'm cupping her ass in my palm.

"Thank fuck for that," I growl as my mouth finds hers.

Every ounce of built-up tension pours from me to her as our lips fuse together.

My hands are all over her body, the concept of being a gentleman or taking things slowly is long forgotten.

I want her, and I want her *now*.

Her hands are making short work of the buttons on the front of my shirt, but it's still taking too long. I reach for it and tug, sending the remaining buttons flying onto the floor and the bed.

I shrug it off and throw it behind me before tugging on the hem of my t-shirt that she's got covering her body.

It's over her head in a flash and I'm staring at her hungrily.

She's got a body made to do wicked things.

She's curvy and full in all the right places, and tight and toned everywhere else.

She's barely covered with a black thong and lace bra, but even those aren't going to last long, not if I have anything to do with it.

She's clawing at the button of my pants and I shove her hand away so I can undo it for her.

I don't even bother taking them off all the way, instead just pushing them down around my thighs – it doesn't feel like there's time to remove them entirely.

I'm beyond frantic.

She shimmies her underwear down her legs as I watch from my position above her, my hard dick in my hand as I reach for a condom from beside my bed and slide it on.

I've heard of foreplay, I swear I have, but I don't think either of us needs it today.

I lower myself down and push into her in one fluid stroke.

"Jackson," she moans, and it's the best thing I've heard all week.

CHAPTER FOUR

Katie

I sit the note down on the bedside table before slipping out of his room, my heels and bag in my hand.

I hope like hell that the place down below doesn't open until evening, or I'm about to do one hell of a public walk of shame.

I probably should have woken him up to say goodbye instead of escaping into the morning light, but I get the feeling the last thing he needs is another woman giving him any kind of drama.

It sounds like he's got enough of that on his plate already.

I creep down the stairs and am met with silence, which is a *total* relief.

I smile as I think about having to lug him up these steps last night as he muttered this and that about his ex.

I don't know a single thing about this Lizzie chick other than her name, but she must not be quite right in the head, either that or the guy she cheated on Jackson with must be a freak in the sack, because *my god*, this morning was amazing.

I haven't had sex that good in a long time. It was more hard, fast and to the point than it was long and teasing, but it was more than satisfying – for both of us.

Even though I know it's never going to happen, I can't help but imagine what it would be like to be with him again, once the lust-filled haze wore off and we could really take our time.

A man like Jackson knows exactly how to use what he's got.

I reach the front door and push it open, the cool morning air hitting me in the face.

I don't even bother putting my shoes back on before looking around for the cab I called.

If you're going to do the walk of shame, you may as well do it right, and besides. I'm not actually ashamed in the slightest.

***

Tillie sips on her takeaway coffee and glances over at me suspiciously as we stroll down the pier.

"You look like you got laid."

I shake my head at her total lack of tact. "Well that's because I got laid."

"*What*? When?! Ew you didn't have sex with that wasted dude, did you?"

I laugh. "Actually, I did... but this morning, when he wasn't drunk at all."

She holds her knuckles out for a fist bump. "Get it, girl."

I laugh again. Tillie always has me in stitches.

"Was he hot?"

"Mmm hmm," I reply as I sip my hot chocolate. I can't stand coffee. Not even the smell of it.

"*Hot* hot?"

I groan. Tillie has always insisted on using this ridiculous grading system of hers that's utterly ridiculous.

"Please god, no."

"Face?" she prompts, not having a bar of my objecting.

"Brad Pitt fifteen years ago," I say with a roll of my eyes.

"Oooo." She nods in approval. "I do love a good Brad."

I sip my drink again and pray that she's done.

"Body?"

"Ryan Gosling. *At least*. Actually, he's probably more Chris Hemsworth."

"Dayummm."

"Voice?"

I shake my head. "I don't freaking know, Tils, okay? For the love of god, he was hot alright. A total dreamboat."

She pouts. "At least tell me if he was packin'?"

"Please tell me you're not seriously asking me about the size of his dick?"

"It's like you don't even know me at all sometimes." She shakes her head in disappointment.

I ignore her and speed up my walking pace.

"You know I'm just going to keep nagging until you spill about the goods..." she calls as she jogs to catch up with me.

She's not even kidding. She's like a dog with a bone when it comes to getting the goss.

"He had a very nice penis, okay? Very functional. Did the job well," I inform her.

She claps her hands together in a slow, show of appreciation.

Sometimes I curse the moment I met Tillie Green. I *really* do.

"When are you seeing him again?"

"I'm not."

I resist the urge to roll my eyes.

"What? Why not? If he gave you the flick, I'll go down there and kick his ass. No man drops my girl like a sack of potatoes."

I laugh and cover my eyes with my free hand. "Seriously, Tills, you need to do something about all of this pent-up rage."

She opens her mouth, no doubt to spill out some more ridiculous nonsense, but I cut her off.

"He's just broken up with his fiancé because she cheated on him. He wasn't looking for anything more than a good time, and neither was I. We had fun. That's all there was to it."

She pouts again and grumbles something under her breath that I don't catch.

She rests her hand on her hip and shoots me a less than impressed look. "So, it was just a one-night stand?"

"Well technically it was a one-morning stand, but I think the sentiment is still the same."

"I do love a good morning roll in the hay... start the day with a bang." She sighs. "Are you sure you won't go back? He sounds kinda perfect. Hot... well equipped..."

I roll my eyes in response.

Tillie has been trying to set me up with my 'dream man' for years now, but she's the only one of the two of us that's concerned about it.

I'm not looking for a guy. I'm happy doing my own thing, and if one day the right one comes along, then so be it.

She's a hypocrite anyway, it's not as though she's even got herself a man.

Tillie is the most single and ready to mingle person I've ever known.

"I'm sure, Tills, he's not looking for a repeat performance any more than I am. *Trust me.*"

CHAPTER FIVE

Jackson
Four months later

"Are you coming out with me tonight?"

I don't even look up from the order sheet I'm filling in. There's no way I'm going out tonight, and neither is he.

He already knows this, yet every god damn Saturday night he's rostered on, he insists upon asking this stupid fucking question.

"Yeah, I'll be there, save me a drink," I answer sarcastically.

"C'mon, boss man, let's shut the place down at eleven and go out on the town."

"Stop talking. Even you aren't going out with you tonight."

"When did you get so old and boring?"

I check the contents of the box that has just been delivered and look up at my best mate with a glare.

"It's true what they say, you know? You should never, *ever* hire your friends."

Bryn chuckles and shoots me that smug fucking grin of his.

It's the one he uses to get the girls — they seem to come running towards a hint of arrogance, but it sure as hell isn't doing anything for me.

I don't know how I've survived this long with this idiot as my head chef. If it weren't for the fact that he's the best on this side of the country, I would have dropped him a long time ago.

"Go do your prep before I kick your ass."

He waves around a kitchen knife like some type of wannabe ninja and gestures for me to come at him.

"Seriously, dude, have you even heard of health and safety?"

I'm trying not to be amused by him, I really am, but it's fucking hard — the guy is the class clown that never grew up.

"I'm going out front. To do some *actual* work. You might be unfamiliar with the term, but give it a try."

"You really need to get some action," he calls after me.

"Because that worked out so well the last time," I mutter under my breath.

I tried the one-night stand thing, and the chick walked out on me when I was sleeping.

Katie.

I still think about her every now and then... and not just about the sex. I actually liked her. She seemed cool. Like the type of distraction I could've used.

I go out front and start checking over everything that has to be done before opening in an hour.

There's a reason this place is booked solid for over a month in advance. I run a tight ship.

Thanks to my moron of a best mate, we serve the best food in town, and thanks to me and the team I've trained, we have some of the hottest tricks in the country being pulled behind the bar, and table service that is second to none.

Some people come here to eat — some to drink. Some to do both.

People will queue for an hour just to get to try one of our cocktails — they're just that good — and that's not even me being cocky, I'm just being honest.

Matilda will be here in an hour to work front of house and charm the hell out of everyone that walks in the door. People don't often realise just how important of a job it is, but I do. She's worth her weight in gold. She's the first person a customer sees when they walk in the door and the last person to speak to them before they leave.

If people leave happy, they come back. They tell their friends, and then they tell their friends too.

That's how this business does so well. There's nothing quite like word of mouth.

I've built this place from the ground up. It was meant to be the future for Lizzie and me, but instead, it's all I have now. And since I have no control over anything else in my life right now, I exercise my power here.

I flick the sound system on and adjust it to just the right level.

I glance at my watch again.

Almost show time.

***

"Jackson, there's a woman at table three that wants to talk to you about making a booking for a function." Clay leans into my office.

I grin at him. "Does she look newly engaged?"

Weddings are solid gold in this industry. You can add an extra zero to the price tag of our services and nobody bats an eyelid.

"It'll break my heart if she is." He grins. "She's a beauty."

I shut my laptop and stand up. "Well, for your sake, I hope she's single and for my sake, that she's planning a wedding." I chuckle as I follow him out.

I do a quick sweep of the room as I walk out into the dining room. I don't need him to lead me, but he's well trained — he'll introduce me when we arrive at the table and then vanish.

I'm looking at the three people at the table curiously. There's a couple looking very much in love facing my direction and I can almost see them begging me to take their money and help them have the reception of their dreams, but it's the woman with her back to me that has piqued my interest.

Clay reaches the table ahead of me and says something to her that I don't catch. Just as I realise who she reminds me of, she turns to face me.

She doesn't just remind me of her – she *is* her.

"*Katie*?" I ask in surprise.

"Well would you look at that, if it isn't the dreamboat himself? I'm impressed you remembered my name this time." She grins at me, and just like the last time, it lights up her whole face.

She stands from her chair and gives me a hug like we're old friends.

It's bizarre how true that feels.

"What are you doing here?" I ask as I let go of her.

I gesture for her to sit and I join them at the table, sitting in the chair that Clay has magicked up out of thin air.

She points to the couple opposite us that I'd forgotten all about from the moment I laid eyes on her. "This is my friend Tillie and her husband-to-be, Reece."

I extend my hand to both of them. I was right. I did smell a wedding after all.

"This is Jackson Matthews," Katie says, and I can hear the humour in her voice. "And it would seem that he failed to tell me that he owns this place."

"In my defence, I wasn't given much of a chance," I tell her with a smirk.

I can feel the woman named Tillie eyeing me suspiciously.

"So, when did you two get it on?" she asks, her finger pointing back and forth between the two of us.

I eye the woman in front of me curiously.

"Are we ignoring that question?" I ask Katie with a sideways glance.

"We most certainly are," she replies with a giggle.

Tillie pouts.

"It's okay, baby, you know you'll force her to tell you later," Reece, her husband-to-be reassures her, with a grin on his face.

That seems to perk Tillie up again.

"*Anyway*... let's get back to it, shall we?" Katie clears her throat. "These two here are getting married in twelve weeks, because you know, weddings require no planning whatsoever," Katie tells me, sarcasm thick in her voice.

"And where exactly do I fit into all of this?" I ask. "Catering?"

"We want to rent this place out," Tillie answers before Katie can.

'Renting this place out' isn't exactly what we do here, but I'm already getting the distinct impression that Tillie won't give two shits about what we *normally* do.

"We normally offer an offsite catering and bar service..."

"Nope." She shakes her head. "I want the reception *here*."

"In *twelve* weeks' time?" I deadpan.

I hear Katie giggle softly.

Tillie smiles sweetly at me and nods eagerly.

"That's, ah... that's a new one," I say as I rub at the back of my neck awkwardly.

The revenue we collect on a Saturday night – because I assume it'll be a Saturday — is pretty high. Higher than I'd feel comfortable charging, even for a wedding.

"I told you it wasn't going to happen," Katie tells her friend.

"It's not that it *couldn't* work... it's just the cost involved would be high. *Really* high." I wince. "And it would be a tight timeline – you wouldn't have access until the early hours of the morning, the day of."

Tillie looks at Reece, who in turn looks at me. "I don't know how to say this without sounding like an ass... but money isn't an issue here. If you can make it happen, then we're in."

"The *entire* place... in twelve weeks...?" I ask again in disbelief, just in case I've misunderstood in some way.

Tillie looks at me with pleading eyes.

I look over at Katie and she's looking at me with curiosity in her dark brown eyes, and that's all it takes to get me to cave. No matter how much of a pain in the ass it's bound to be, I'll do it if it means I'll get to see her again.

"Well, alright then." I shrug. "Why the hell not?"

I hear Tillie clapping her hands together excitedly, but I can't take my eyes off Katie. She's gorgeous, and she's intriguing.

"I can't believe you got your way *again*." Katie rolls her eyes at Tillie and Reece as they high five each other.

I may have only met these two a few minutes ago, but it doesn't surprise me. They seem like one hell of a power couple.

"I'll get you my card," I tell Tillie as I look around for Clay so I can send him to get one for me.

"You take mine instead," Katie says, and by the time I look down, there's a shiny gold card sitting in front of me.

"You're a wedding planner?"

"She's not just a wedding planner," Tillie tells me, "She's the *best* wedding planner in town."

"I'm the craziest wedding planner in town for agreeing to take on the two of you as clients." Katie laughs.

Tillie smiles sweetly at her. "Oh, that's *cute*. You say it like you had a choice."

I chuckle at their banter. They remind me of me and Bryn.

Clay appears next to me and leans down to speak quietly in my ear. "You're needed in the bar."

I nod and turn back to the table. "I'm sorry, duty calls."

"Send me an email and we'll sort out some details," Katie tells me.

I shake my head at her as I get to my feet. "I've got a better idea, I'll take you to dinner and we'll organise it then."

She smirks at me. "I don't think that's a better idea at all."

"It's a fantastic idea. I'll call you... now that I actually have your number." I wink at her.

"Let's just keep this professional, alright, dreamboat?"

"You can call it a business meeting, Katie. I'll even arrange it in an email if that suits you better... whatever will help you sleep at night."

She narrows her eyes at me, but I can see a smile pulling at the corners of her lips.

"It was great to meet you both. I'll see you soon." I nod at both Tillie and Reece before following Clay out of the dining room.

"Alright, chica, *spill*," I hear Tillie demand as I walk away, and I laugh to myself.

Katie's going to need a fair bit of luck to get through that one.

CHAPTER SIX

Katie

To: Katie North (katie@chasingperfectionplanners.com)
From: Jackson Matthews (matthewjack@gmail.com)

Hey Katie,

I booked us in for dinner at 8pm tomorrow night, next door to my place. Don't even bother trying to tell me you can't make it because you'll only be lying to yourself.

Jackson

To: Jackson Matthews (matthewjack@gmail.com)
From: Katie North (katie@chasingperfectionplanners.com)

Hey dreamboat,

You're annoyingly persistent, did anyone ever tell you that?

Katie x

To: Katie North (katie@chasingperfectionplanners.com)
    From: Jackson Matthews (matthewjack@gmail.com)

Some say I'm as persistent as I am handsome. Am I picking you up or meeting you there?

Jackson
    P.S. Do you give everyone a kiss at the end of an email, or is it just me that gets the special treatment?

To: Jackson Matthews (matthewjack@gmail.com)
    From: Katie   North   (katie@chasingperfectionplan-ners.com)

And modest too...
    I like that you just assume I'm saying yes.

Katie (note the no kisses)

To: Katie North (katie@chasingperfectionplanners.com)
    From: Jackson Matthews (matthewjack@gmail.com)

You wound me. It's a business dinner, dimples, you can claim it as an expense and everything.

Jackson xx (note that I'm willing to give kisses, anytime, anywhere)

To: Jackson Matthews (matthewjack@gmail.com)
    From: Katie North (katie@chasingperfectionplanners.com)

Don't you 'dimples' me, dreamboat. What do I have to do to get you to leave me alone?

To: Katie North (katie@chasingperfectionplanners.com)
    From: Jackson Matthews (matthewjack@gmail.com)

Coming to dinner would be a good start...

To: Jackson Matthews (matthewjack@gmail.com)
    From: Katie North (katie@chasingperfectionplanners.com)

Fine. *One dinner*. And if you try to get into my pants, it'll be your last meal. And I won't be claiming it as an expense, because you'll be paying.

To: Katie North (katie@chasingperfectionplanners.com)
    From: Jackson Matthews (matthewjack@gmail.com)

You women... ALWAYS thinking about sex. Did you know it's possible for a man and woman to be friends after they've slept together?

To: Jackson Matthews (matthewjack@gmail.com)
    From: Katie North (katie@chasingperfectionplanners.com)

Now who's lying to themselves?

To: Katie North (katie@chasingperfectionplanners.com)
    From: Jackson Matthews (matthewjack@gmail.com)

We can be friends, dimples. You'll see.

I'll see you tomorrow at 8. Since you're such an independent woman, I'll meet you there.

Jackson xoxo (even threw some hugs in there because I'm generous like that)

I suck in a deep breath through my nose and blow it out through my mouth.

I can't deny that I'm a little bit excited by the idea of seeing Jackson again. I don't want to be, but I *am*. He's endearing and charming, and far too good looking.

It's quite a predicament.

I have a date that's not actually a date with a man I had a one-morning stand with, and whom I still find incredibly attractive. What could go wrong with that?

***

I step out of the cab at eight on the dot and glance up at the building in front of me.

I smooth down the front of my dress and look around for any sign of Jackson.

I don't know why I'm so nervous. I'm *never* nervous for dates, and certainly not for business meetings, which is what this is meant to be, after all.

It could be the fact that Jackson has seen me naked that's got me on edge, but I don't want to think too much about that right now.

"Dimples!" I hear his voice and I turn to see him walking out of the busy restaurant that's right next to his own.

Everything down here on the waterfront is exquisite. Expensive too. Most of the finest dining establishments are down here. Jackson's place is undoubtedly included in that category.

I didn't tell him — I didn't want to risk stroking his ego too much — but I was seriously impressed with the standard last night.

I'd never eaten in 'The Boat Shed' before, and I'd only been in for a drink one other time — the night I wound up in his bed — and I didn't even know he was the owner back then.

The whole place was perfection. I'm not entirely sure how a man can run a business that runs the way his does, yet have a bedroom in the state his was in.

"Dreamboat." I grin at him as he jogs over to me.

He looks good. He wears his suit like an extension of himself. He's groomed to perfection and carries an aura of confidence that somehow manages not to cross over into arrogance.

"I was worried you wouldn't come," he murmurs as he leans in to hug me, his lips briefly brushing my cheek.

The contact, as quick as it was, still gives me tingles.

"Well, I heard the food is really good here, so I figured I could endure an evening in your company for the sake of the cause," I offer with a grin and a shrug.

He chuckles and dips his head before holding his hand out to me. "We better get in there then."

He leads me through the door without a second glance from the big guy out front who is turning people away in droves, past the woman at the front who offers Jackson a flirty smile and earns herself a scowl from me, into the busy dining room and over to a table that's right next to the glass with the perfect view of the water.

I stare out the window for a moment; it's absolutely breathtaking.

"Not a bad spot, is it?" Jackson asks as he pulls out my chair for me.

"It'll do I guess." I smirk.

It's the best table in the whole place. I have no idea how he got it on such short notice.

"The owner owed me a favour," he answers my unasked question as he pours us both a glass of red wine from the bottle that's on the table.

"Oh yeah?" I ask as I take a sip from the glass he's offered me.

I almost moan in appreciation. It's an unbelievable drop.

"Gabriel, the owner, forgot his wedding anniversary last month. I got him a table at the last minute and she was none the wiser to his little slip of the mind."

"And you called in your return favour for *me*?" I tsk at him. "*Silly*... you should have saved it for a hot date."

His eyes find mine and he stares hard. "You're the only hot date I've had in a long time."

I swallow deeply, trying to push down the lump in my throat. "Were the others all ugly then?"

He chuckles and the intensity in his eyes dims a fraction.

"There hasn't been any others. Dating hasn't really been on my radar."

I sip my wine again. I don't know what to say. I've only been on one date myself lately, but it wouldn't have mattered if he'd just admitted to going on one hundred, it's the intensity I can feel radiating from him that's got me on edge.

"Why'd you run out on me, Katie?"

It's not what I expected him to say at all. In fact, I was hoping I might have got away with not talking about it at all.

I clear my throat nervously. "I thought you'd prefer it that way... you had a lot going on. I didn't want you to have to ask me to leave, so I just made it easier..."

It sounds lame when I say it aloud, but I really meant no harm by walking out that morning. I didn't do it to hurt or punish him in any way. I just didn't want him to feel any pressure.

He had enough going on without having to say an awkward goodbye to some girl whose name he barely knew.

"What if I wanted your number?" he presses.

"You weren't ready for my number. You told me yourself you were still in love with your ex." I shrug. "Speaking of, how's that going for you these days?"

"I'd be lying if I said I was over her completely," he answers honestly.

I give him a look that says 'my point exactly'.

He grins at me and just like that, he's back to being the Jackson I recognise. "You know what? I've come to the conclusion that we should be friends."

I sip on my wine again and swirl the glass around as I watch him and his cheeky grin.

"You don't want to be friends... you want to be friends with benefits."

He chuckles and leans back in his seat. "Well, now that you mention it, a few benefits never hurt anybody."

"Not happening."

"What about if I ask you again in the morning?" He grins suggestively. "I know how much you like things in the morning."

I roll my eyes. "*Friends*, dreamboat, that's it."

I'm not even entirely convinced that I *wouldn't* sleep with him again given half a chance, but my voice sounds far surer of my point than I really am.

He holds up his hands in surrender. "Alright, dimples, *friends*."

"Why do I already feel like I'm going to regret this?"

He winks at me mischievously.

CHAPTER SEVEN

Jackson

I wave over the waiter and hand him the empty bottle of wine. Our second for the night. "Another of the same," I tell him.

"Nuh uh." Katie shakes her head at me. "No more, dreamboat. I'm tapping out."

She points a finger at the young guy who's now holding the empty bottle of wine and looking between the two of us to see if he should bring another bottle. "Do *not* bring us any more," Katie tells him.

"*One* more." I wink at her.

"*No more*," she demands.

She turns her attention from me to the waiter, snapping her fingers at him. "Hey, *Justin Bieber*, we're done. If Ken doll over here has another one, I'll end up having to carry him up the stairs again and, quite frankly, he's heavy."

"Yes, Ma'am."

She gestures for him to come closer and he leans in. "And between you and me, I'm not sure I can be trusted in his bedroom if I've got any more wine in me."

I chuckle as he nods his head at her rapidly and scuttles off, a big grin on his face.

"Party pooper." I scowl at her.

"Some of us have to work tomorrow," she says in a sassy tone.

We've both had a few at this point and I know damn well we don't need any more, but I'm not ready for this evening to be over just yet. I don't want to have to say goodbye to Katie.

"You want to come next door with me and we can talk about this wedding?"

She raises a brow at me. "*Oh,* so you did plan to actually do something work related tonight?"

I chuckle. I'm not even going to try and deny that I've hi-jacked this entire evening. I had no intentions of talking work. I would rather talk about her.

"I'll tell you what, I'll come next door if you promise to show me a photo of this Lizzie chick."

I chuckle. *This Lizzie chick.* "Oh, you mean the woman who ripped out my heart and stomped all over it?"

"If we're going to be friends, you're going to have to stop laying it on so thick with the theatrics," she says with a roll of her eyes.

"You asked."

"I want to know what she *looks* like, not that you and your tiny little violin are still pining away for her."

"Harsh, but fair." I grin at her.

I thought I'd imagined her being so easy to talk to and be around, but I didn't. She's relaxed and funny, she's smart and open, she's witty and charming, and as much as it's an inconvenience to me and our new friendship arrangement, I can't deny that the woman is sexy as hell.

All night my mind has been pulling up memories of her naked and beneath me.

I can almost hear her soft moans in my ears.

But she's right. I'm not over my ex and she's not the kind of girl that's going to go for a friends with benefits kind of arrangement.

My choices are limited, but clear — for now at least.

I want to be around her, I know that much for certain. Everything seems brighter when she's around, so I guess we'll be friends.

I'm not sure how I'm going to coach my semi-hard dick through that one, but I guess I'll just have to figure it out as I go.

"Let's get out of here," I announce. "I need to put my violin back in its case."

***

"This is her?"

I nod. "That's her."

She looks at the picture again and huffs out a breath. "*Well,* weren't you two just the full Ken and Barbie package. Did she drive a pink convertible?"

I chuckle as I sit down on the couch and put my feet up on the coffee table.

"*No*... it was red."

Katie rolls her eyes.

"Quite the rock she's got on her bony little finger there too," she observes.

I laugh at her bluntness as she joins me on the couch. "She didn't like the ring I chose her— we had to go back so she could pick a replacement... That one really hurt the wallet."

"What a *bitch*!" She gapes.

She's like sunshine mixed with a little hurricane. She's sweet and kind, but at the same time she's sassy and strong. I get the feeling she's the kind of woman you want *on* your side.

She tosses the photo onto the coffee table as though she's seen quite enough of it and turns her attention to me.

"So... Did she give it back?"

I frown at her. "What? The ring?"

"*No*, the bony finger..." she rolls her eyes again, "*yes* the ring, that thing looks like it cost enough to feed a small village."

I shake my head. "I didn't want it back."

The last thing I need is that stupid ring lying around here reminding me of what I had.

She gapes at me. "You are a *total* sucker. What's her address? I'll go get it back for you. And I'll only keep fifty percent of what we can sell it for." She makes a move like she's going to go and do exactly that.

I grab her arm and pull her back down. "You're crazy." I chuckle.

"I'm practical," she argues with a grin.

"I'm not telling you where she lives."

"Oh c'mon... what about forty percent, but I get to rough her up a little bit?"

"You're not just crazy, you're bat-shit crazy, dimples."

Her face breaks out into an even wider grin.

"Made you smile while you were thinking about her though, didn't I?" She shrugs at me with a smug smile.

"How do you *not* have a boyfriend?" I ask her.

I know it sounds like a pick-up line, but I don't care. I genuinely want to know. She's a complete catch. It's hard to believe that no one has snapped her up already and put a ring on her finger.

"Who said I didn't have one?"

I try not to let the panic seep into my features. Here I am — suggesting that we be sex buddies — and I never even had the decency to ask her if she was in a relationship, I just assumed she wasn't. I'm such an ass. It seems to be a common theme where Katie is concerned.

I wince. "*Do* you have one?"

She smiles at me coyly and makes me wait for an answer. "*Relax*, there's no big burly boyfriend that's going to come kick your ass. It's just me."

I'm relieved, even though I know it's unfair of me. But I only just got her to agree to be friends; I'm not ready to share her yet.

"I think I'd be more scared of *you* anyway."

"I knew there was a smart man hiding in there somewhere."

I clap my hands together and move my feet from the table as I sit up straight. "So, you better tell me about this wedding..."

She smirks at me. "Nice try, dreamboat. I want more info on Malibu Barbie over here."

I groan. "She ran off with my mate, what more is there to tell?"

There's *everything* more to tell — I know that, but I don't particularly like talking about my heartbreak. I torture myself with it enough inside my head without having to say it out loud.

"How'd you meet?"

I contemplate walking across the room and smacking my head against the brick wall of my living room, but I think better of it.

I'm pretty sure Katie would still expect answers, concussion or not.

"We met in a bar."

She huffs out a laugh. "Ironic."

I nod in agreement.

"How long had you been together?"

"Five years total, engaged for two of those."

"Wow." She mouths the word.

Wow is right. Lizzie threw away years of our lives and our entire future without so much as a backwards glance.

"This 'mate' of yours..." she makes air quotes on the word mate, "how long had you been friends?"

"Since high school." I almost growl. "You know, I think he's always had his eye on her. He was with me the night that I met Lizzie, and I swear in some fucked up way he thought he was righting the course of fate — like he should have been the one to get her number that night and it should have been his five years with her instead of mine."

"That's fucked up," she blurts out and I can't help but crack a smile.

She's shaking her head solemnly.

"It's fucked up," I agree.

"Did you at least get to punch him in the face?"

I chuckle now. "I wanted to. But no, I've got a reputation and my business to look after, and he's not worth risking that for. He's taken enough — I won't give him the satisfaction of seeing me lose that too."

"Would you take her back if she came knocking tonight?"

My laughter dies down nervously. "You're not afraid of asking the hard questions, are you?"

"Should have been a journalist," she quips, but she doesn't stop looking at me, or waiting for her answer.

"Does it make me sound like a loser if I say I'm not sure?"

"Hmmm..." she thinks about it for a minute, "I don't think it makes you a loser... A fool perhaps... But you loved her — you clearly still do — those feelings don't just go away."

"You sound like you're speaking from experience..."

She shrugs and wraps her arms tighter around the couch cushion she's holding to her chest. "Not really... I mean, I think we've all had our heart broken at one point or another, but there's no crazy ex-fiancés hiding in my closet."

I nod my head as I think about the truth in that. Everyone has lost something in their life.

"You must be doing a bit better at least... It looks considerably better in here than it did last time."

She's back smiling again, and just like that, we're done with the deep and meaningful.

"You caught me at a bad time. I promise I don't normally live like a homeless person."

"And no empty photo frames in sight. I might even be impressed."

"I aim to please," I drawl.

"You know, maybe this friends thing could work out after all. I kinda like you."

"You reckon you can tolerate me?"

"We'll see." She giggles as she reaches for the giant planner she's set down on the coffee table. "I'll make the final decision after we see how you deal with bridezilla's demands."

I grab my tablet and swipe open the screen. "Let me guess, she's been planning her dream wedding since she was six years old."

"I wish." Katie huffs with a roll of her eyes. "More like she got engaged six weeks ago after knowing the guy for about a month, and she's never even thought about a wedding in her *entire* life. I would literally kill for a six-year-old girl's wedding scrapbook at this point."

"A *month*? Jesus Christ, can anybody say shot-gun wedding?"

Katie laughs and her eyes twinkle. Those dimples that I'm beginning to really like are on full display.

"You know what, *that* I would understand, but she's not even pregnant. Just *insane*."

I open up my booking schedule. "Alright, give it to me — what does the princess want?"

Katie starts rattling off the list and I make a mental note to send Reece a bottle of scotch, because holy shit, he's going to need it.

CHAPTER EIGHT

Katie

I grab my phone and tap out a text message.

To: Jackson
  From: Katie

Dreamboat, I need a favour.

I really need him to agree to this to save my sanity. Not that I'm entirely sure he's the best thing for my sanity. The man is enough to drive anyone insane. These past few days, he's been like a bad smell I can't shake. I don't really want to shake him if I'm being honest — I'm enjoying his company and conversation too much.

To: Katie
  From: Jackson

Sexual or other?

I snort out a very unladylike laugh at his response. It's what I've come to learn is a classic Jackson reply.

To: Jackson
    From: Katie

Other. Jesus Christ, you really need to get laid.
    Tillie and Reece are making me go play mini putt and I need you to come.

To: Jackson
    From: Katie

PLEASE

To: Katie
    From: Jackson

Mini putt? Do people still go to mini putt? I didn't know that was a thing for people over the age of 10.

To: Jackson
    From: Katie

Well apparently it is. C'mon... please? If I have to use those stupid mini clubs then so do you.

To: Katie
    From: Jackson

What are you going to give me if I agree?

To: Jackson
    From: Katie

Anything that's not a blow job.

To: Jackson
    From: Katie

OR SEX. Jesus, that was close.

To: Katie
  From: Jackson

Spoil sport.

To: Jackson
  From: Katie

PLEASE! If you don't come, Tillie will have Reece bring some boring dude from his office to set me up with and then you're going to have to listen to me whine about that for at least a week...

To: Katie
  From: Jackson

I'm rolling my eyes. Where and when?

I grin victoriously at my phone as I give him the address and time.

I'm far more excited about Tillie's stupid plan now than I was fifteen minutes ago, and I know that's got everything to do with the fact that Jackson will be there to keep me company.

***

"I should warn you," Jackson says with a grin as he tosses his arm around my shoulders. "I'm somewhat of a mini putt prodigy."

"Oh, I'm *sure* you are," I reply with a roll of my eyes.

He grins as though he's perfectly at home here with me and my friends.

"I should probably warn you that Reece nearly turned pro as a golfer."

"Pffft." He chuckles. "That's golf, dimples, this is mini putt... completely different ball game."

"That's entirely inaccurate."

He just winks at me as he lifts his arm off my shoulders and heads off to go and study the course.

I'm not sure how he plans to work out a game plan for the spinning windmill, or the clown mouth that opens and shuts, but I get a really good view of his ass when he bends, so I'm not about to point out the flaws in his tactics.

Tillie skips over to me, a less-than-impressed looking Reece trailing behind her.

I cover my mouth and laugh yet again at his appearance; he's wearing his full golf gear and he looks like a total nutcase that dressed up like a pro to play mini putt.

He catches me laughing and points a warning finger at me. "She pulled me off the golf course for this."

"Don't blame me." I hold my hands up in surrender. "I'm here under duress too."

Tillie bats her lashes innocently at her fiancé. "You're always telling me that you'd love me to play with you."

"On the *green*, baby."

"There's some green right there." She points at the fake green on each section of the mini putt.

"God damn, you're lucky I love you," he mutters as he stalks off in the direction of Jackson.

"Love you too, baby," she calls after him, a smug grin on her face.

"You better not drive that man away. I don't know how he puts up with all your crazy," I tell her, my eyes still trained on Jackson, who is now discussing strategy with Reece.

"I like to call it charm."

"Whatever helps you sleep at night," I muse.

"What about you, huh? That sexy piece of meat helping *you* sleep at night?" She waggles her brows at me suggestively. "You sure seem to be seeing a lot of him."

"Oh terrific," I drawl, "we've upgraded from annoying to sexist."

She laughs and nudges my elbow with hers. "Don't try and change the subject."

I nudge her back. "I sleep like a baby at night, thank you very much."

She looks Jackson up and down. "Oh, I bet you do."

I roll my eyes and ignore her remarks. There's no convincing Tillie of anything once she's made her mind up, and I'm not going to waste my time trying.

"*Happy Gilmore*, you ready?" I ask Reece with a grin as I approach the guys and the first hole.

"That's *it*. I'm going home," he announces.

Tillie giggles and wraps her arms around his neck. "Don't worry, baby, I think you look sexy as fuck."

That gets a smile out of him and before I know it, they're kissing each other so passionately that I have to look away.

"Looks like you're up first, dreamboat," I say as I take my club from him.

"Are you sure I can't tempt you into a make-out session too?" he asks with a raised brow.

"As enticing as that sounds, I think I'll take a rain check."

He drops a ball on the ground in front of him and lines it up with his club as he looks down at the hole.

"You know what... We should put a bet on this game."

I roll my eyes at his back. "Just hit the ball already."

He straightens up and turns around to face me again. "I'm serious. Let's put a wager on it."

I sit my hand on my hip. "Alright, what do you want?"

"You. In my bed," he says with complete conviction.

I feel my cheeks burn. "Is that the only way you can get laid, by winning a bet? That's kinda sad."

"Beggars can't be choosers." He chuckles.

I'm not entirely sure if he's serious or not, and I can't help but admit that a part of me would like to lose that bet.

"Relax, dimples, I'm kidding." He grins.

"Oh, and here I was, all set to shake on it," I say, doing my best to hide the relief in my voice.

He chuckles and lines up his ball again.

"You know what I think?" he says without looking up at me.

"Enlighten me."

"I think I won't need a bet. I think you'll fall in love with me all on your own one of these days."

I shake my head at him and his nonsense. "I am only a mere human after all," I say with a roll of my eyes.

He might be hot as hell, but I'm not anywhere near falling in love.

He taps the ball with his club and it ends up nowhere near the hole he was aiming for.

I pat him on the shoulder and give him a shove to the side. "Out the way, *Tiger Woods*, let me show you how it's done."

***

"I can't believe I left golf early for *this*," Reece grumbles as Jackson crouches down to try and line up his shot.

"Oh, don't be mad, baby, no one is judging you for your crappy score," Tillie tells him.

"Your score was even crappier," I point out. "And she's lying to you, Reece, we're *all* judging you."

Jackson chuckles and stands up straight again. This is the fourth time he's crouched down and muttered to himself about angles, and quite frankly, I'm bored of it now.

"Get on with it already. We all know you're going to miss," I bait him.

It's his final shot. If he makes it, then we're tied for the lead. If he misses, I win.

"It's not his fault he can't get it in the hole," Tillie pipes up. "Common problem, Jackson, don't sweat it."

"I'll have you know, I have no problem at all getting it in that particular hole," Jackson retorts, a grin on his face as he studies the shot yet another time.

"*Seriously*," I groan at their sexual innuendos. "If you don't hit it in the next thirty seconds, I'm going to take that ball and shove it up your—"

He taps the ball and my words are cut off as I watch it roll down the green path and hit the wall before bouncing off and heading straight for the hole at the end.

It goes in with a clunk and I hear myself groan loudly.

"How you like them apples, dimples?" Jackson asks, a wicked grin on his face as he prowls towards me.

"Yeah, yeah, nice shot, but you still didn't win," I say as I sit my hands on my hips like a sullen teenager.

"I know. But neither did you, so mission accomplished." He smirks.

I pout at him.

"It's not all bad, we can share the trophy."

He laughs at my expression as he throws his arm over my shoulders again.

"Let's get out of here," he suggests as he steers me towards the exit. "Reece has had a rough day — I think he could go for a beer."

"I could go for a change of god damn clothes, that's what I could go for," Reece mutters, and I can't help but laugh.

Who would have thought mini putt could actually be fun?

CHAPTER NINE

Jackson

"What's going on with your face?" Bryn demands.

I scowl at him. "What the fuck is that meant to mean? It's my face. There's nothing wrong with it."

He narrows his eyes at me sceptically. "Well, you look weird. Like smiley and shit."

"Thanks very much, man," I mutter as I check another thing off the list in front of me. "You're doing wonders for my self-esteem."

"I aim to please," he quips with a bow. "Now, back to business... are you ready for me to ruin your day?"

I groan. "Not particularly. Can it wait until later?"

"Not really, but I do have some good news as a side dish of sorts."

"Hit me with the Brussels sprouts first," I tell him as I close my folder with a loud clap.

"Maddy is sick. She can't come in tonight."

"*Motherfucker.*" I groan. "We open in an hour, couldn't she have let us know earlier in the day?"

He shrugs at me. "She only just started puking, what do you want me to do about it?"

I rub my temples. "How come you got the job of delivering the bad news anyway? Where's Clay?"

"I literally got the short straw. We drew for it." He shrugs.

"Sucks to be you," I drawl. "I'll take that side dish of good news now thanks."

"I've got the *perfect* fill in." He grins as though he thinks he's some kind of genius for thinking of whoever this dream replacement might be.

"Tick tock, bro," I tap my watch, "you want to spit it out or what? I'm pretty sure you've got cooking to do."

"*Katie*." He crosses his arms across his chest and gives me a look like 'I've nailed it, right?'.

"I don't think so," I say with a shake of my head. "I'll have Kim do it, and I'll get Rachel in to cover her shift."

"Rachel is on holiday," he answers without missing a beat.

"Alexis?" I ask hopefully, even though it's becoming clear that either him or Clay have already explored every other possible avenue.

"Broke her arm last night at basketball."

"Jesus Christ."

"So, do you want to call Katie or should I?"

I groan.

"C'mon, man, she'll be perfect."

"How on earth do you know she'll be perfect? You've never even met her."

"Clay said she was hot, and you're always harping on about her, so I figure she must be a bit of alright."

I wrack my brain trying to think of a solution that doesn't involve me ringing up Katie and begging her to come in here and save my ass.

"You're coming up blank, huh, boss man?" he says smugly.

"I could do it myself."

"You're pretty enough, but you have that weird face thing happening, so maybe not."

I flip him the bird.

"Besides, you're on the bar tonight, remember... you told Stu you'd cover for him until ten?"

"God damn, when it rains it fucking pours."

"Call your girl already and quit your whining."

I sigh and pull my phone out of my pocket. "Yeah, yeah... I'm calling her — but she's *not* my girl."

He says something smart that I don't catch.

I walk away until he's out of air shot and hit the call button. It rings four times before she picks up.

"Miss me already?" she teases, her voice soft and warm.

I chuckle nervously. "Umm.... yeah, something like that..."

"Why do I get the feeling you want something from me?"

"Probably because I want something from you."

"Cashing in your favour so soon?" she says, and I can hear the smile in her voice.

"I'm afraid so... but the good news is, it's not a blow job I'm after."

***

"I'm really sorry to ask you to do this."

She smiles and shakes her head. "Honestly, it's not a problem. I'm actually kinda excited to play host."

"Well, hopefully you won't have any problem customers and it'll all be smooth sailing."

She reaches out and grips my forearm lightly. "Jackson, *relax*, I'm only doing the basics... People come in, I get their names and have someone take them to their seats. When they leave, I ask them how they liked the food and I take their money. It's not exactly rocket science."

"Don't forget to smile."

"I'll be utterly charming. You'll see," she tells me with a wink. "Now get out of here, you're cluttering up my entry."

She dismisses me with a wave of her hand, and suddenly I'm not sure who's in charge of who anymore.

"I'll be at the bar if you need me."

She doesn't look up from the computer screen in front of her. "Not going to need you, dreamboat."

I shake my head. I don't know what just happened. I got told.

I slink behind the bar. I can see her in full view from here, so at least I'll be able to keep an eye on her as I make drinks.

She looks up from the screen and glances around the room until her eyes find mine. I wink at her and she gives me a wave.

I watch Clay walk over to the front door and push it open to let the queues of people that will be waiting outside, in.

I can see a group of women that look suspiciously like they're on a hens night heading directly for the bar.

"Alright, boys," I say to the two other bartenders who are behind the bar with me, "buckle up, women wearing penis headbands are never a quiet evening."

***

"You got eyes on you, boss," Jeremy, one of my servers tells me as he sidles up to the bar with an empty tray.

"Whose eyes?" I ask as I load up the batch of cocktails I've just made. I hope to god it's not that group of hens again; they were way too excited and drunk enough that I'm not willing to serve them any more tonight. I feel like a hypocrite given some of the states I've got myself in at this very bar — but that's the perks of being the boss.

"Whoever that chick is working the front.... and *damn*, man, is she replacing Matilda?"

I glance up at Katie and find that she is in fact looking my way. I give her a smile and shake my head at Jeremy. "She's just filling in."

"That's too bad. I could have got used to looking at her."

I chuckle at him and his young naivety. "You're only saying that because Matilda won't go out with you."

His cheeks turn crimson. "How'd you hear about that? Can no one around this place keep a damn secret?"

"You told Bryn, man... *Everybody* heard about that."

He mutters something under his breath that I don't catch, and I chuckle at his pissed-off expression.

"Don't blame it all on Matilda," I tell him. "I bet Katie won't go out with you either."

"Thanks for the pep talk, boss." He huffs as he picks up the now-full tray.

I sneak a peek at Katie again and find that she's watching me with a smile playing on her lips.

I mouth the word 'hi' to her and she mouths it back.

I make a gesture like I'm having a drink and point at her. 'Thirsty?" I mouth across the room.

She nods her head eagerly.

I grab a bottle of vodka from the top shelf and toss it in the air before catching it again and pouring a shot of the clear liquid into a tall glass in front of me. I toss the bottle again, making it spin in the air over my head, and catch it behind my back.

I throw a few of my best tricks until her perfectly-made drink sits in front of me.

"Show off," I hear one of the guys mutter.

I glance up to see if Katie caught my little performance, and given the way she's staring with her jaw lax, I'd say she saw it alright.

"I'll be back in five," I tell them as I round the front of the bar, snagging the glass as I go.

"You didn't tell me you were part magician." She gapes at me as I hand her the drink.

"I'm full of surprises. You've got no idea."

She takes a sip and moans softly. "Maybe I should come here more often."

"If you want to see more of me, you only have to ask, dimples."

She rolls her eyes at my lameness. "Your jokes are terrible, but this cocktail is delicious."

I take the compliment and ignore the insult.

"You coping okay over here?"

I can already see that she's been coping just fine.

She's a natural. She's good with the customers, she can problem-solve and she's hot as hell — which isn't actually a requirement of the job, but it certainly doesn't hurt.

"I'm fine." She beams up at me.

"You know that it's customary to stay after shift for a drink, right?"

"I have work in the morning."

"It won't be too late. We'll be closed by midnight tonight."

She chews on her bottom lip for a moment as she deliberates. "You're a terrible influence, you know that, right?"

"I think you might have mentioned that once or twice." I feign innocence. "Bryn wants to meet you, and I owe you after tonight... *Please*?"

"Fine," she says with a resigned sigh. "But if I'm hung over tomorrow, I'm blaming you."

CHAPTER TEN

Katie

My phone chimes again from inside the drawer of my desk, and I finally give in and pull it out to check it.

I don't know who it is, or what they want, but they're persistent, I'll give them that.

If it's Tillie wanting to know which shade of off-white I prefer for her wedding colour scheme, I just might kill her.

I'm not in the mood for annoying humans today, I'm tired — thanks to staying up late with Jackson and his staff, and quite frankly I'm a little hung over — also thanks to Jackson and his stupid bottles of delicious red wine.

Much like our first dinner a few weeks back, it's become clear that Jackson is very partial to a bottle of red.

We've been spending a fair bit of time together, mostly under the guise of planning Tillie's wedding, but honestly, his part is pretty minimal at this point. I just like hanging out with him. It's fun and easy, even if he does seem to lead me astray more often than not.

"Annoying bad influence," I mutter under my breath as I look at the screen of my cell phone.

I hold back a string of curse words as I see that I have twelve new, unread messages. All from the gorgeous, pain-in-the-ass himself, Jackson Matthews.

To: Katie
  From: Jackson

Meet me for a drink tonight? No red wine this time, I promise.

To: Katie
  From: Jackson

Dimples, you there?

To: Katie
  From: Jackson

If I don't get a reply in ten minutes, I'm going to assume it's a yes.

To: Katie
  From: Jackson

Katie?

To: Katie
    From: Jackson

Has there been an alien invasion and they've taken your body to be a host?

To: Katie
    From: Jackson

Katie?

To: Katie
    From: Jackson

I'm going to call you instead.

Notification: One missed call from Jackson Matthews

To: Katie
    From: Jackson

You're going to kill me when you see all these texts...

To: Katie
   From: Jackson

"But I won't stop, and I can't stop..." How's that Miley song go, dimples?

Notification: Two missed calls from Jackson Matthews

I groan and let my head rest against the desk. I don't want to be even slightly amused by this ridiculousness, but I am — just a little tiny bit. I haven't even managed to read them all yet, but I've seen enough to last me a long time.

I hit dial on his number before he has the chance to send me yet another annoying message.

"Dimples!" he answers brightly, "I was just about to send out a search party."

"You're a total nutcase, you realise that, right? You sent me like a dozen texts, Jackson, and you got the words to that Miley song wrong too. You seriously need to get a hobby for your days off."

"I hear what you're saying, and I'll take your suggestions on board."

"We've only been friends for a few weeks and you're already driving me insane, who did you annoy before I came along?" I ask him as I lean back in my chair, a grin already on my face.

"I think you just bring out the quirky side of me."

I huff out a breath. "*Quirky*? Is that what the kids are calling it these days?"

He chuckles deep and long, and I curse myself for smiling even wider at the sound.

He's just *too* likeable. He might be a crazy, ex-obsessed guy who drinks a little too much — but I like him. I'm comfortable around him and that's not a typical thing for me.

"What do you even want, dreamboat? There were so many messages I can't even recall where it started."

"Don't play hard to get with me, dimples, we're going out for drinks."

I snort laugh. "*We* are not. I have plans tonight."

"So, cancel them."

I can hear the smile in his voice — the smug little shit.

"And why would I want to do that?"

"Because you got a better offer," he replies, his tone cocky.

I smirk and twirl my chair around so I'm looking out the window. "I did? Funny, I can't say I recall getting a better offer."

"You ignore me all morning, and now you just drive the knife in even deeper." He groans in mock outrage.

"I was working!"

I shake my head, a stupid grin on my face. He might be a pain, but I enjoy this banter we have going.

"I'm not coming out with you, dreamboat, you drink too much."

"Oh c'mon, my shout?"

"*Tempting*," I muse, "But it's not happening. You're on your own."

"Spoil sport."

"Seriously, go check Google for AA meetings in your area," I tease.

"You're mean."

"No, I'm *honest*."

He laughs, and I can't stop myself from laughing along with him. "I'll have to get Bryn to come keep me company."

"I'm definitely not coming then. I'm not sure who would drive me crazy faster, you or your sidekick."

"I'll call you tomorrow."

"Just the one time would be great."

"I make no promises." He chuckles before the line goes dead.

I smile at my phone for a long time before I realise what I'm doing.

Jackson Matthews is a distraction that I don't have time for right now. A sexy, funny, sweet, distraction, but still a distraction nonetheless.

***

"Tillie, Jesus, you cannot have *every* surface covered in flowers."

"Reece says I can have *whatever* I want," she replies smugly.

"Well *Reece* isn't the boss here, I am. *Christ*, you're lucky that man adores you, because you are twenty kinds of crazy with these wedding plans."

She pops another carrot in her mouth and chomps down on it.

"And seriously, eat some real food would you, the last thing we need is for you to go on some stupid wedding diet and have to have your dress altered at the last minute."

She smirks at me. "I'm going to have Reece pay you more, you look overworked and underpaid, sweetie. And besides, I haven't even got a dress yet."

I take a deep breath in through my nose and blow it out through my mouth, as I try to reign in my temper.

Tillie might be my best friend, but she is quite possibly the most high maintenance bride I've ever had to deal with.

She wants it all. *Everything.* And she needs it on short notice. And then she changes her mind at the drop of a hat and decides she wants something completely different.

She's got a loaded husband-to-be who wants to give her every last thing that she wants and tells her that she deserves it all — which is not helping the situation in the slightest.

He's not wrong, she *does* deserve to have the perfect day, but that day is *not* going to include a full brass band and one hundred doves being released.

No way in *hell.* Not on my watch.

"I'm going to have Reece cut up your credit card," I threaten.

She shakes her head and smiles at me like I'm a naïve child. "Oh, sweetie, I've got about ten of the things."

Tillie had no idea how much money Reece had until the day he proposed to her, so no one can technically accuse her of being a gold digger... but she certainly hasn't shied away from the lavish lifestyle he's offered her, in fact, if anything, she's dived in head first.

"Can we just get back to the flowers?" I beg. "This might shock you, but you're not my only client."

"Fine. Halve the order." She pouts.

I sigh. Halving the order still means there will be flowers absolutely fucking everywhere, but at least we'll actually have space for the guests now, and the florist won't have to work the entire week before to arrange them all, so I try to think of it as a win.

"So, what's the deal with you and Jackson? You've been hanging out an awful lot..."

I scrawl down a few notes about decorations before dropping my pen and reaching for the bowl of French fries on the table.

"Yeah... We're friends."

"I wish I had friends that looked like that."

I laugh and nearly choke on my mouthful of food.

"We're *just* friends, Tillie, it doesn't matter how he looks."

"Friends with benefits, at least, I hope? God knows you could do with a few benefits," she says dramatically.

"Just friends. No benefits."

She raises her brows at me.

"Well one benefit. Once. But you know that was before we became friends."

"I'm just sayin' is all." She picks up another friggin' carrot and points it at me. "You know what you're missing out on."

I *do* know *exactly* what I'm missing out on, but I also know that giving in to temptation would be a bad idea. Jackson is hot, there's no denying it. But he's also still very much messed up over his ex, and that's a drama I don't need.

I shove the bowl of fries at her. "Eat something with calories, all this health food is messing up your brain."

She frowns at them like they're toxic and takes another nibble of her carrot.

"So, you're telling me you don't like him?"

"Of course I like him. You know I do."

"So, you don't find him attractive then?"

I roll my eyes at her. "Don't be ridiculous. The man could start a fire just by looking at it, he's that hot."

She shoots me a knowing look.

"Some of us are in control of our sexual urges."

"Some of us are full of shit," she retorts.

Friends with benefits is exactly what Jackson keeps hinting at — actually forget hinting — he flat out suggests it, at least once every time I see him.

It's a private joke of ours at this point, so I don't take him too seriously, but I also know full well that he wouldn't say no if my answer suddenly changed from no to yes either.

I could tell Tillie that, but I won't. The last thing she needs is any encouragement on this particular topic.

"I'm going to go call Reece and tell him to run while he still can." I make a show of picking up my cell phone. "If he goes now, he just might get away unscathed."

She giggles and finally takes one of the fries from the bowl.

"Where is your new BFF tonight anyway?" she asks.

"Went out drinking with his mate from what I can gather."

"Let's hope he winds up wasted and needs someone to take care of him then, huh?" She crosses her fingers in front of her face, all the while grinning like the smartass she is.

"He's still in love with his ex, Tills, nothing good would come from the two of us sleeping together again."

"I can think of something good that might happen. It starts with 'or' and ends in 'gasm.'"

I can't help but laugh at her. My best friend sure is one of a kind.

"And besides, that was months ago, wasn't it? Surely he's moved on by now?"

"They were together for five years, *and* engaged. Those feelings don't go away just like that." I snap my fingers for emphasis.

"Oh, *sure* they do." She waves her hand dismissively. "He just needs to find himself a hot Chica like you."

"I bet your fiancé would be so pleased to hear you say that," I drawl.

"If my fiancé keeps it in his pants and doesn't go screwing around with my friends, then we won't have a problem, will we?" she replies, full of sass.

"Touché." I giggle.

I hear my phone ring and look down to see who's calling me at this time of the night. I hold up the phone to show Tillie the screen; it's flashing 'Jackson Matthews'.

"Well, speak of the devil."

"Hello?" I answer.

"Dimples, I did something stupid..."

He wasn't kidding when he said he was going drinking. He sounds toast, and it's not even midnight yet.

"I tried to stop him, Katie," I hear a guy yell in the background.

"Sshhhh, *I'm* talking to *Katie*," Jackson scolds the person in the background as he puts major emphasis on my name.

I giggle. "Who is that?"

"Bryn. He bought tequila shots." He gags a little bit at the mention of the word. "He cooks with a hat on," he informs me helpfully.

"You boys sure like to go full noise, don't you?"

I mouth the words 'they're wasted' to Tillie.

She gives me a thumbs up like it's the greatest news she's heard all day.

"Are you going to tell me what stupid thing you did?"

"Mmm hmm... We were at a bar... Then Bryn wanted to go get burgers."

"*You* wanted to get burgers, *I* wanted a kebab," I hear Bryn yelling at him.

"Whatever, man, you're holding a cheeseburger. Don't yell at me about kebabs."

I cover my mouth with my hand in an attempt to muffle the sound as I laugh at the two of them.

I can hear them walking in a way that can only be described as a drunk dude walk. Their footsteps are heavy, sloppy and slow and Jackson's breathing is laboured.

"Jackson! Just tell me what you did."

"He went to—"

"Shhhhh! I'm gonna tell her *myself*," Jackson hisses at Bryn.

"Whatever, bro, I'll just eat my *burger*," I hear Bryn tell him.

Tillie has scooted around the table now and has her ear pressed up against the phone so she can hear the nonsense for herself. She's almost got tears running down her cheeks, she's laughing so hard.

"Katie?" Jackson asks suddenly.

"Yeah, dreamboat?"

"I thought you were gone." He sighs in relief.

"*I'm* still here, but where did *you* go?"

"I went to go see Lizzie."

I give Tillie an 'I told you so' look and she rolls her eyes.

"I told him it was a stupid idea," Bryn yells to me.

I hear a thump and an 'ow'.

"I hit him," Jackson announces proudly.

"He should be the one hitting you for going to see your ex. Put him on the phone so I can ask him to knock some sense into you," I demand.

"I'm drunk, dimples," he says, totally ignoring me, and I can hear the warm, happy, drunk glow in his voice.

"No shit," I mutter under my breath. "So, was Lizzie home?" I ask, and I'm not sure which answer is the one I want to hear.

"Nope," he replies, popping the 'p'. "And I knocked for aaaagggges. Woke up her neighbours and everything."

I hear a suspicious-sounding burp from the background.

"Dude! Are you spewing?" Jackson yells into the night.

"No, I'm *not* spewing. I just threw up in my mouth a *little* bit," Bryn replies.

I rest my hand against my forehead and try not to laugh. Tillie isn't helping in the slightest — she's in hysterics.

"Where are you two knuckleheads?"

"Oi, Bryn?"

I hear no reply.

"I think he *is* having a spew," Jackson tells me with a laugh.

Even now, drunk as a skunk, his laugh still makes me smile.

"Oi, B... B! Where are we?"

I hear some murmuring that I can't make out and then Jackson produces a surprisingly specific-sounding location.

"I'll tell you what, if you two sit the hell down, I'll come and pick you up, alright?"

"You're the best, dimples."

"I'll see you soon. Try *not* to get in any trouble while you wait."

"I *told you* Katie would save me," I hear Jackson telling Bryn before I get a chance to hang up the phone. "She's hot *and* she's nice."

I burst into laughter.

"Oh Jesus, now *that* was entertainment," Tillie says as she wipes the tears from the corner of her eyes.

"Grown-ass men." I giggle with a shake of my head. "C'mon...We better get out of here before B1 and B2 get themselves lost."

CHAPTER ELEVEN

Jackson

"Katie!" I say as I peer into the open window of the car that's stopped at the curb. "You came."

She laughs and shakes her head at me.

I'm *drunk*. I know I am.

Not as drunk as I was when I decided to go knock on my ex's door, but still drunk nonetheless.

"Get in, lover boy," a voice that's not Katie's tells me.

"Tillie the bridezilla, you came too." I grin at the woman who I hadn't even noticed until she spoke.

Katie covers her mouth and laughs.

"I really like your laugh, dimples," I tell her as I lose my balance a little bit and wobble into the side of the car.

"I'm glad you like it, now do you maybe want to get in before you fall down?"

I nod at her, because it sounds like a good idea. She always has good ideas.

"Where's your mate?"

I turn and try to remember the last place I saw him.

"He's here somewhere," I tell the girls.

"Bryn!" I yell into the quiet street.

He doesn't answer. I turn back to the girls. "He's a li-abi...li...liabil...lia-bil-ity." I finally get the word out.

"Is he now?" Katie giggles. "I can't imagine what that's like to deal with."

"What are you yelling about?" I hear Bryn call from behind me. "I was just taking a piss on some flowers round back."

"Oh *lord*," Tillie says.

"What'd I tell you..." I say, matter of factly. "*Liability*." I smile proudly. I'm impressed I got it right this time.

"Alright boys, in the car, before you get yourselves arrested."

I shove Bryn as he approaches, and he shoves me back, but somehow, we both make it into the car unscathed for the most part.

"Seatbelts, gentlemen, and if either of you puke in here, you'll be paying for a valet, got it?"

"Yes, Ma'am," I tell her with a salute.

We drive for a bit and I can feel my eyelids getting really heavy.

"Katie?" I hear Bryn say.

"Yeah?"

"I don't cook in *just* a hat. I wear pants and a shirt too. I just wanted you to know that."

Tillie is laughing at him. Katie might be too.

"Thanks for clearing that up for me," Katie tells him, and yip, she's *definitely* laughing.

"No problemo," he replies. "Oh, and Katie?"

"Yes, Bryn?"

"Jackson is drunk off his ass, but he's right, you *are* hot and nice."

"Fucking told you," I murmur before I feel myself drift off to sleep.

***

I wake up feeling like I've been hit by a bus, then it's backed up and run me over again just for good measure.

Drunk me obviously didn't shut the curtains, because the light is streaming in and hitting me like a slap in the face that I really don't need.

"I have *got* to stop drinking like this," I tell myself with a moan.

"You and me both," a voice says and makes me near jump out of my skin.

"Jesus Christ," I say as I roll over and find a pair of feet near my head. "What the fuck are your dirty feet doing on my pillows?"

Bryn's head pops up from down the end of the bed. "Didn't you get the memo? We're top and tailing."

I rub my temples to try and settle my pounding head. "What the actual fuck? Did we get drunk and turn into teenage boys on a school camp?"

"I'm never drinking tequila ever again." Bryn groans as his head falls back to the pillow.

A flash of Bryn and I stumbling down along a familiar street flashes in my head. "Oh shit," I mutter. "I went to Lizzie's."

"*We* went to Lizzie's," Bryn corrects me. "Your stupid ass made me an accomplice."

"Why the fuck didn't you stop me?"

"I tried, man, but you're a big dumb idiot when you've got a few shots under your belt, and to be completely honest with you, I kinda wanted to see you finally yell at the bitch," he says with a yawn.

I throw up a silent thank you to the universe that she wasn't home. I don't know what on earth would have possessed me to go around there last night, but thankfully, I managed to dodge a bullet.

Another memory floats into my mind of Katie calling me dreamboat and telling me I was an idiot.

"Oh *Jesus*, I called Katie."

"Yeah ya did." He chuckles. "Who do you think tucked us into bed?"

"Oh shit, not again. I seriously owe that woman."

"Hey look, she left me water and pain killers," Bryn muses as he wiggles around in the bed, moving his feet far closer to my face than I'd like them to be.

"She's good like that," I say as I swat at his ankles.

"She's cool, man. I like her."

I like her too. I'm surprised about just how much. I like her more than I probably should, but I know myself, and I'm not ready for anything new, no matter how hard it's becoming to stay convinced of that.

I hear Bryn chugging back his water. "She's like an uber driver with perks."

I find myself smiling even though embarrassingly enough, this is the second time that Katie has had to deal with my drunken ass. We haven't known one another long, but I can hardly remember what it was like before we were friends.

I roll over to see if she's left me anything to fix my raging headache.

I've got water and pain killers too, and also a note that I can't open fast enough.

Dreamboat,

1. *You're an utter moron. Don't even argue, because you know it's true.*
2. *Seriously, check out an AA meeting — I was joking the first time, maybe not so much now.*
3. *You know what, maybe you should keep drinking after all, you're kinda funny when you're drunk.*
4. *Nope, cancel that, you're a moron.*
5. *Visiting your ex, what were you thinking?!*
6. *Did I mention you were a moron?*
7. *You just told me I was your best friend and that I have pretty hair. Drunk you is actually pretty sweet.*
8. *You owe me lunch, and make it a good one, you can pick me up at 1.*

Love Katie (the hot and nice girl) xx (and yes, those are kisses, but only because you're drunk)

"The woman is a saint," I mutter.

Bryn sits up on the bed and holds his hand out for the note.

I hand it to him.

"Remind me again why you're just friends with this chick? She's fucking awesome," he says as he scans the letter.

She *is* awesome, and if it weren't for my stupid ex-fiancée turning my heart bitter and black, I'd be going after Katie. But I'm all fucked up, so it's better that we're just friends, no matter how badly I'm starting to want her.

"Have you forgotten how my last relationship ended?"

He tosses the note onto the bed. "Are you *still* milking that thing?"

I scoot up so I'm sitting against the headboard. "If by 'that thing' you mean my future wife sleeping with our mate and then leaving me, then yeah, I'm still 'milking it.'"

"So, nothing is going on with you and Katie?"

"Nope."

"And you don't want to be anything but friends?"

I avoid his eye and lie through my teeth. "Nope."

I've been hanging out with Katie a lot lately, and the attraction between us is only growing stronger every time I see her. It's harder to resist her with every passing day.

She's a beautiful woman, but I can't give her more than sex, and I don't want that for her — for us. She deserves more than just a fuck buddy.

"So, you won't mind if I ask her out then?"

Every muscle in my body is tense, because the idea of my best mate and Katie going on a date is so fucking terrible, but instead of manning up and telling Bryn the truth, I shrug my shoulders and reply, "Sure, do whatever you want."

***

"Well hello there, sunshine, don't you just look like a box of fluffies," Katie tells me with a smirk. "How's the head?"

She does up her seatbelt and smiles at me wide and smug.

"It's been better," I admit sheepishly as I pull out into traffic.

"Oh, that's an *understatement* and you know it. I have to admit, I'm a little disappointed I didn't come out with the two of you after all, you boys seem to know how to party."

I can tell she's on the verge of laughter already.

Bryn and I have done a fine job of making a mockery of ourselves, it would seem.

"Would you believe me if I said I was never drinking again?"

"Would you believe me if I said I was the Queen of England?"

I chuckle. I can feel her looking at me as I drive, and I peek at her out the corner of my eye.

She looks entirely too appealing — my pounding head is not capable of contending with the urge to touch her right now.

"Where are we going for lunch?" she asks brightly, clearly enjoying my misery. "Somewhere loud and filled with children?"

"You're *so* funny," I reply sarcastically.

"Oh, don't forget 'hot' and 'nice' too." She's biting down on her bottom lip to try and stop herself from laughing, and batting her lashes at me innocently.

Unfortunately for me, she looks anything but innocent, she looks *tempting*.

I make an executive decision to keep my eyes on the road for the rest of our journey.

CHAPTER TWELVE

Katie

"Where are we going?"

I've been watching out the window, but I'm not familiar with this stretch of road at all. We're snaking along the coast, the road running alongside a stunning view of the ocean.

"We're almost there. It's my favourite spot; it's the reason I opened my restaurant by the water."

I sit up a little straighter and try to see what he's talking about. I'm intrigued about where we're going, he's a pretty open book with me, but physically getting to see something that inspired him first-hand is an exciting concept to me.

He slows the sleek black car and flicks on his indicator.

We turn down a narrow gravel road and drive until we almost reach the shore.

He turns off the engine and grins at me. "Alright, dimples, out you get."

I glance around as I step out of the car, I can see how it would be inspiring out here, it's beautiful and untouched.

Right now, I feel like we're the only two people in the world.

I hear him shut the boot of the car and I see that he's holding a picnic basket and blanket in his hands. It's all very sweet.

"No screaming children out here," I observe with a smile.

He winks at me. "I'm not just a pretty face after all."

He might be joking, but he really does have a pretty face. Especially out here in the light ocean air; he looks like he's come home.

"Down that path." He points with his elbow.

I offer to take something from his full hands, but he just shakes his head at me and smiles his gorgeous full smile.

I wander down the path, feeling like a child who's experiencing their first trip to the beach.

This is nothing like the beaches I normally frequent. Those beaches are covered in people and full of energy.

This is the polar opposite. We're the only ones here and I've never heard such peaceful silence.

I can hear waves softly crashing against the shore, and the faint squawk of seagulls in the distance.

We reach the end of the overgrown path and come out onto the warm golden sand.

I reach down and kick off my shoes. I run down to the water's edge and watch as the water washes over my toes.

I laugh and spin around in a circle.

This place is incredible.

I stop spinning so I'm facing Jackson and find him still standing back by my shoes, watching me with an intense curiosity.

"This is beautiful," I call out to him.

"*You're* beautiful," he calls back.

It should feel like a cheap attempt at flattery or like a cliché pick-up line, but somehow it doesn't.

I've never heard more genuine words in my life.

He sets down the basket and toes off his own shoes.

I can't take my eyes off him. I wouldn't have thought it was possible for tension to build over such a distance, but apparently, I was wrong.

I can feel the caress of his eyes on my skin, almost as though he's actually touching me.

I watch with bated breath as he follows my footprints through the sand until he's standing right in front of me.

"This is my little piece of paradise," he murmurs as he reaches a hand out slowly to cup my jaw.

We're blurring the lines of our friendship right now, but I don't have it in me to think about stopping it.

There's *something* between us. We both know it — it's what we choose to do about it that will define what happens from this point on.

"It feels different with you here," he says, his tone hushed, even though we're the only people around.

"Good different or bad different?" I whisper.

"Everything is better when I share it with you."

The water is washing around our feet as we stand here, locked in a silent standoff in a perfect setting that feels so far from the real world.

Maybe that's what it is — the fact that none of this feels real — that makes it okay for our lips to meet in the softest of touches.

My hands tentatively reach out to grip his shirt as his mouth moves in sync with mine.

The kiss is so passionate, yet tender, it's hard to imagine ever stopping.

When we do finally break apart, he's breathing so hard you'd think he'd just run a mile.

"Where did that come from?" I whisper as he rests his forehead against mine.

"I don't know," he whispers backs, "I just know when I'm with you, everything glows."

***

"Oh my god, Bryn might be a genius after all." I moan in satisfaction as I peek into the last of the containers he's brought out here for us.

"If there's one thing he knows how to do other than talk shit — it's cook," Jackson replies from his spot on the blanket.

He's got his sunglasses on, shirt off and is lying flat on his back, soaking up the afternoon sun.

I've perved at him far more than I'd care to admit, but it'd be impossible not to; he's gorgeous, and that confidence he radiates is making it impossible for me to look away.

"It suits you out here."

I look at him in surprise. I can't see his eyes through his dark shades, but I assumed they were closed, not watching me.

"Thank you for bringing me, you've definitely made up for last night."

He grabs the bottles of water from next to him, tossing them out of the way, and gestures for me to come and lie down next to him.

I lay myself down and stare up at the light clouds moving lazily across the sky.

"I don't know what I was thinking going to see her last night."

"I think the tequila might have been doing the thinking for you."

"I'm really sorry, Katie," he surprises me by saying.

"For what?"

I reach my hand up in the air and draw around some of the shapes I can see with my finger. I can feel him watching me.

"For getting drunk again, for calling you... For going to see Lizzie..."

"You don't have to apologise to me for any of that — you don't owe me an explanation."

"I know I don't have to, but I want to."

I don't know what to say to that. I don't want his apology. If I'm honest with myself, I'm not sure what I want.

"If anything, you should apologise for taking a piss on the tyre of my car when I got you home," I joke in an attempt to lighten the mood.

This man here next to me isn't the playful Jackson that I've gotten used to these past few weeks, this is a more serious version that's lying at my side, and I'm not sure how to approach him.

It's like being out here has stripped away his barriers and defences.

"Christ, I pissed on your car? I really am sorry."

"You also told me that we should be like Mila Kunis and Ashton Kutcher," I say with a giggle.

He chuckles. "What the hell does that even mean?"

"I might be wrong, but I think you were referencing the movies that they both did about having friends with benefits – separate movies might I add – but the sentiment was there."

"Maybe I meant we should get married and have a couple of kids," he teases.

"Oh yeah, I'm sure that's where you and your drunk penis were going with that conversation."

"I'm not sure my penis was drunk." He chuckles.

"What was it doing peeing on my car then?"

"Touché." He laughs deep, and I feel the vibration of it against my side.

"You know what, dimples, I think meeting you might have been the best thing that's happened to me in a really long time."

I know he means having me as a friend, but my heart isn't quite getting the message as it pounds a thousand miles an hour in my chest.

I know myself well, and I know that I'm falling for Jackson, if only just a little bit.

I'm hypothetically teetering on the edge of the cliff face. Right now, only my toes are hanging over the edge, but I know it'll only take a slight breeze for the rest of me to follow.

He lifts his arm over my shoulders and I lift my head to rest on his bare shoulder.

"We better get back soon, it'll start cooling off."

"Do we have to?" I whisper. "I could stay here forever."

I want nothing more than to stay here with him where it's just the two of us and nothing else matters.

I know that things will go back to normal when we leave this beach, and I'm okay with that — if it were real between us, it would exist everywhere, not just here in this secluded paradise — but I'm not sure I'm ready to give it up just yet. I want a few moments more.

"I wish we could too," he whispers as his fingers trace light patterns on my arm.

I close my eyes and breathe in deeply; I want to absorb this afternoon and every single thing about it right into my soul.

We lie there together for what feels like an eternity longer, tracing cloud shapes and laughing together before he announces that it's finally time to go.

He holds my hand all the way back to the car and then we drive back to an unwelcome reality.

***

It's been two days since we kissed at the beach, and it's almost as though it never even happened. If it weren't for the sand in my shoes and the sunburn on my shoulders, I might have believed that I imagined the entire afternoon.

I don't know if I'm thrilled that there's no lingering awkwardness between the two of us after we crossed that line, or if I'm devastated that it didn't lead to anything more.

Jackson isn't ready for anything more, so I guess it's all for the best in the end that we're still friends after throwing caution into the wind.

I'm happy with the piece of him that I have. He's quickly become such an important part of my life. He's the person I want to tell when something funny happens to me, or when I get a new client. He's the first person I text in the morning and the last person I text at night.

If Tillie keeps acting like such a nightmare bride, I might have to get Jackson to replace her as my best friend entirely.

"Are you even listening to me?" the nightmare bride in question snaps at me as she holds out two handfuls of lilac fabric that are so close to being the same colour, at a glance you wouldn't even notice the difference.

"Not even a little bit." I say with a yawn.

I'm *exhausted*. We've been at the bridal studio for over two hours, and all we've established so far is that Tillie wants an off-white dress, and I'll be wearing lilac.

"The wedding is in six weeks, Katie," she tells me, her tone full of outrage.

"I'm well aware, Tills, *trust me*."

Her eyes widen, and she looks like she's about to erupt into a full-blown panic attack.

"Breathe," I demand. "Step away from the colour swatches."

She drops the fabric and takes a deep breath.

"Now go over to that wall and pick a dress to try on."

"I wanted custom-made."

I smile at her sweetly. "Well bad luck, honey, like you said, we've got *six* weeks. The best these ladies can do for you is to find something off the rack, and then have it altered so it's exactly how you want it, okay?"

She huffs out a breath. "What if—"

"No amount of money is going to help this time, Tills. I told you to start thinking about a dress weeks ago."

"Well you could have told me I needed to actually listen to you," she says with a pout.

"Well for the record, from now on, how about you just listen to me all the time, mmkay?"

My patience is wearing seriously thin at this point and I have to keep reminding myself that she's my best friend, and I'd be here dealing with her theatrics whether I was her wedding planner or not, but it's becoming increasingly harder and harder not to shake her and tell her to pull her head in.

She looks over at the wall lined with dresses. They aren't just 'off the rack' chain-made dresses. These are all handmade, one-of-a-kind dresses, but I don't have the patience to go through all of this with her again.

"I'm being a diva, aren't I?" she asks with a wince.

"That's an understatement," I mutter.

"How badly do you want to slap me?"

"My palms are literally twitching," I say, as I do my best not to crack a smile.

"Do you want to just smack me once to make you feel better?" she asks with a poorly concealed grin.

I take a deep breath and the corner of my mouth twitches with a smile. Tillie's back. She's still fucking crazy, but it's her normal level of crazy, not the possessed version of her that's been present all morning and for eighty percent of the time these past few weeks.

"Or I could ask Reece to pay you more?" she offers as she scrunches up her nose at me.

"You're going to send that man broke." I say with an amused shake of my head. "How about you just go try some of those dresses on and promise to never threaten me with purple fabric swatches ever again?"

"They're lilac, you animal," she tells me with a wide grin.

"Don't start with me again," I say with a laugh.

She flicks through a couple of dresses on the rack and pulls one out for closer inspection.

I turn to the dressmaker, who is virtually hiding in the corner, give her a thumbs up and usher her to get the hell over there. If we can tame the beast while she's feeling relaxed, then this day will go a hell of a lot smoother.

She scuttles over to take the dress from Tillie, and I make a mental note to have Reece give her a generous bonus.

"You can pay me back one day and turn into the bride from hell when you get married," Tillie says as she hands the terrified-looking woman another dress.

I snort out a laugh. "Let's not get ahead of ourselves now shall we. I don't even have a boyfriend."

"Oh, sure you do," she muses as she strolls into the changing room, "you just don't know it yet."

CHAPTER THIRTEEN

Jackson

"So, we'll need to set up the table for gifts and the flower wall over here." Katie points out a section of the back wall.

"*Flower wall*?" I raise my brows at her in question.

"Don't even ask," she warns.

I laugh but don't ask anything more. I don't have a clue what a fucking flower wall is going to involve, but I'm way out of my depth here.

One thing I do know, is that Katie has the patience of a saint. I don't know what keeps the woman going amongst all this madness. Nothing seems to rattle her past the point of what she can handle.

She knows exactly who she is and what she's capable of and it's an incredible thing to watch. She's not afraid to say what she thinks or do what she wants, and I envy that about her.

I can barely admit things even to myself.

The way I feel for Katie for example... Something has changed between us since that day at the beach. I'm feeling things I'm not ready to feel.

I still feel so messed up over everything that happened with Lizzie, I can't possibly consider starting something new.

Katie is nothing like Lizzie, but this isn't so much about her as it is about me.

I'm the one with the crutch here, and the last thing I want to do is hurt her, or even worse — lose her.

I felt it that day I kissed her at the beach too — what was at stake — it all flashed before my eyes, exactly what it was I had to lose.

I don't know how I ever thought we could be fuck buddies. It would *never work*, she's too utterly *intoxicating*. Once or twice with her would never be enough.

I want to know *everything* about her, but even with that desire burning bright inside of me, I know I'll never succeed, she's too complex of a creature — she's always changing and evolving. She's always learning and growing.

She's nothing short of inspiring.

Nothing in my life might be progressing right now — my business has reached its peak, my relationship has failed, yet I've never felt less static in my whole life. Katie's taking me along for her ride and I can't do anything but hold on and try to grow with her.

"And over there will be the lanterns with the string lights."

"Of course," I reply as I'm pulled from my inner thoughts. "It wouldn't be a wedding without string lights and lanterns."

She ignores my sarcasm and carries on circling the room with her enormous planner in her hands.

"So, the guests will be invited up here right after the ceremony on the pier, and we'll serve drinks and canapés right away."

I nod.

"Are you writing this down?"

"Drinks. Food. I got it. I think we can manage. But just back it up a few steps, they're getting married on the pier?"

She nods her head and rolls her eyes.

"Do I even want to know how they got approval for that?"

I've owned this business for years, and I've *never* seen a wedding on the pier before. Not once.

"Reece took care of it — I didn't even want to know what he had to do to make that happen," she informs me as she scrawls something down — some minor imperfection that she'll straighten out, no doubt.

"You know, dimples? I think I should make friends with Reece. He sounds like a useful guy to have around."

"He might not appreciate a friend like you." She smirks at me as she finally pulls her eyes from her work.

"What's wrong with my friendship skills?" I demand, putting on a show of sounding wounded, even though I know damn well all the dirt she's got on me.

She shrugs. "I mean, *nothing*... If you like being called in the middle of the night drunk as a skunk, or propositioned for sex... Or getting five hundred texts while you're trying to work."

I roll my eyes. "You exaggerate. It was only about two hundred."

"Fine, *two hundred*." She grins. "But my argument still stands."

"I see where you're coming from... He wouldn't be able to handle all of this."

"I don't quite know how I manage myself," she drawls.

"Oh c'mon, you know you couldn't live without me."

She doesn't answer, just smiles coyly and walks off in the direction of her best friend and most difficult client.

***

"Here, you deserve one of these." I pop the cap and hand her a cold beer.

She's out on my balcony, staring out at the sun setting behind the horizon.

"How did I not know about this view before now?" she asks as she takes the bottle from my outstretched hand.

I take a sip of my drink and shrug. "I dunno. Have you been here when it's not dark or I'm not drunk?"

"It would seem not."

"Another black mark against my friendship skills." I sigh.

"You're sure racking up those indiscretions, aren't ya?" She smirks before taking a long drink of her beer.

I rest my elbows on the railing and look at the sunset.

"That's the best thing about moving in here. I get to look at that whenever I want to."

"It's not a bad outlook, is it?" She sighs. "Where'd you live before?"

"Lizzie and I had a house downtown. She still lives there actually. That's where I went that night," I admit sheepishly.

"Is she still with the guy, your mate?"

I shrug. "You'd like to hope so. Since it ended an engagement *and* a friendship."

"You hope they're still together?" she asks in disbelief.

I chuckle and shake my head. "Nah, not really. I hope they made each other miserable within the first three days and now they're both desperate and alone."

"That sounds more like the Jackson I know and love," she teases.

I'm shocked into silence by her casual use of the word. I know she's not out here declaring her undying love for me or anything like that, but I haven't heard anyone tell me they love me since Lizzie lied to my face and then screwed around with my mate behind my back.

"So, what was the plan?" she asks me, totally oblivious to my little moment. "For your life I mean... You were obviously going to get married. Did you want kids?"

I shake my head. "Lizzie didn't want kids."

"I didn't ask what *Lizzie* wanted," she says softly. "I asked if *you* wanted to have children."

I think about it for a moment before realising that children is something that *could* be a possibility for me now. Lizzie never wanted them — she made that clear from the day we met. I didn't think I was too fazed one way or the other, so I just accepted that we wouldn't have them. It's not until right now, when Katie has asked me what *I* want, that I realise I *do* want kids one day.

"One day... I think one day I could be a good dad."

"What about getting married? Or has she put you off ever trying that again?"

"I don't know." I shrug.

I haven't really thought about any of this until now, and while if anyone else was asking these questions, it would feel like an intrusion, with Katie is feels natural. Like she's part of my thought process.

"I guess it would depend on the person and the timing. I think I'd know if I found the right person and it was the right time to ask that question again."

"What about this place? Any big dreams you want to tell me about?"

I shrug and take a long pull from my bottle. "I'm not sure. I mean I guess I've always had plans to expand and build on from this, but I'm not sure about any of it anymore."

"How long are you going to let this hold you back for?" she asks, and it's not an accusation, it's a genuine question. Her voice sounds sad, like it pains her to see me holding onto something that's over and done and causing me nothing but grief.

It's a weird thing, breaking up with someone you thought you'd spend your life with.

I can see the cracks in our relationship now that I'm looking back, but at the time, she felt like everything I'd ever wanted or needed. I thought we were solid.

I don't know if it's feelings, or pride or something else that's holding me back from letting go of all that hurt, but I just can't seem to release it entirely — I'm not even sure if I want to or not.

Maybe that's the problem.

Maybe it's me.

"She's still got control over you, because you're letting her. Holding onto your hurt isn't affecting *her*, Jackson, it's only affecting *you*. The only person you're punishing is yourself."

She sits her empty bottle on the handrail next to my arm and leans in to kiss me on the cheek.

"I'll see you tomorrow," she whispers before she turns and leaves.

I stay out there for a long time after she's gone — even though I know I have things to do downstairs — and think about the truth in her words.

CHAPTER FOURTEEN

Katie

"Listen up, I want you to be prepared for anything here, just brace yourself, alright? She could turn on any of us at the drop of a hat."

Jackson chuckles at me. "We're going through menu options, not handling a baby dinosaur."

"Trust me, dreamboat, at this point they're one and the same."

He looks at me as though I've lost my mind, but he'll see soon enough what I'm dealing with.

"I hope you had Bryn make plenty of food, she's been living off carrots for the past two weeks and the woman is *hangry*."

"You're overreacting."

"You're under-reacting."

"That's not a thing."

I hear the door open behind me and I glance over my shoulder to see Tillie strolling in.

"Oh, *trust me* it's about to become a thing."

He just laughs at me and waves out a hello to Tillie before disappearing into the kitchen to safety.

"Chicken shit," I mutter under my breath. "Good morning, how's my most difficult client doing today?" I ask Tillie sweetly as she approaches.

She rolls her eyes at me and pouts. "You make me sound like I'm hard work or something."

"That's because you *are* hard work, sweetie. Now, where's your man? I was relying on his presence to keep you sane."

"He's running late." She frowns, and I send up a silent prayer for Reece, that Tillie gets some carbs into her before he shows up, because he's bound to get a tune up for not arriving on time.

"Sit," I instruct. "Jackson has gone to get some samples."

Surprisingly, she sits without arguing. "Lover boy better be bringing me something good," she grumbles.

I look around for Jackson, and when I catch his eye across the room, I tap at my wrist, indicating that he should hurry the hell up.

We have the whole place to ourselves. It doesn't open for another hour yet, so it's just us and Jackson's staff here.

I can hear Bryn banging around in the kitchen and Jackson gives me a thumbs up and a cheeky grin.

I can't help but smile. I'm turning into a total sucker for that man and I don't even think I care anymore.

That's the thing about chemistry and relationships. You can't force it and you can't help the way you feel about someone, so there's really nothing more to do than hold on and see where the ride takes you.

"You've got a goofy look on your face." Tillie says as Jackson approaches, holding a tray of something that is bound to be delicious.

"And you've got a resting bitch face," I tell her with a poorly concealed giggle.

She's about to say something smart in retaliation, when Jackson arrives and slides the tray in front of Tillie.

"How's my favourite bride doing today?" he asks her.

I roll my eyes at his obvious ass kissing.

"You could learn a thing or two from this guy, Katie," Tillie tells me as she eyes up the plate of food.

Jackson rattles off exactly what the choices are while I watch Tillie practically dribbling.

"Eat," I tell her. "I'll get you a glass of water."

I stand up and wink at Jackson as I leave him alone with my best friend.

He shoots me daggers and then plasters a smile on his face before turning back to Tillie.

I make it about halfway across the dining room when I hear a 'psssst' noise.

I glance around but come up empty.

"Pssssst." The noise goes again, but this time I see a grinning Bryn inside the doorway of the kitchen. "Katie!" he whisper shouts, "Come here."

I walk over to where he's lurking, studying him curiously as I go. "Did you just 'pssst' me?"

"That's not important, what *is* important is getting that stupid fool over there to open his eyes."

I stand in front of him and cross my arms over my chest.

Bryn is an intimidating guy, if for no other reason than the sheer size of the man. He's *huge*, but I get the impression he's a big teddy bear on the inside.

"What exactly is it that he's opening his eyes to?"

"You," he says, as though it's the most obvious answer in the world.

"*Me*?" I reply loudly.

"Shhhhh," he hisses as he drags me a little further inside the door frame. "He's so obviously into you."

"I'm pretty confident that that is entirely inaccurate," I retort.

"I told him I was going to ask you out," he says with a wide grin, as though that's some kind of explanation for this bizarre conversation.

He's backed me up so that my back is pressed against the door, and he's leaning over me as he talks in a hushed voice — his toned bicep isn't far from my face and his hand is resting against the wall next to my head. He's effectively blocking me off from the dining room.

I look up at him. "No offence, but I think that'll be a no."

He chuckles softly. "You cut me deep, Katie, but that's not what I mean. I'm only doing this to make him jealous."

"He's got no reason to be jealous, Bryn, so there's a slight flaw in your genius plan."

He shakes his head at me as though I'm stupid. "Look, let's quit beating around the bush. Are you into him, or what?"

"Yeah, I've got feelings for him, but I'm not going to use those feelings to pressure him. That's not how I work. I don't play games, I don't manipulate."

"It's not manipulating, it's just like a gentle slap across the face," he says with a shrug and a grin.

"Well you can slap him all you like, but I'm not doing it. I *like* Jackson, I like where we're at. I just want him to be happy and the rest will just be whatever it will be."

"Don't you just want to shake some sense into him?"

"Of course I do sometimes, but *not* so that he'll decide he loves me all of a sudden."

"So, you won't go out with me to try and make him jealous?"

"That would be a negative."

"Well he's looked over here at least half a dozen times already so maybe we don't need the date."

"Bryn!" I scold him as I shove at his chest to get him away from me. "Get back in that damn kitchen, stop making trouble and start making some food."

He salutes me like a soldier as he walks backwards into the kitchen.

I hear him start whistling and banging around and I take a deep breath.

Mother of god.

I just confessed to having feelings for a guy — to his best friend, who seems to have a mouth that's considerably too big, and I'm not sure what I'm going to do about that.

I don't want to pressure Jackson *or* lose our friendship. I like what we have. I like that I can talk to him about anything, and that he'll tell me things no one else has ever heard.

The last thing I want is for him to be pressured into feeling something he isn't feeling. He's still hung up on his ex, and that is what it is. He won't be ready to move on until he decides he's closed that chapter of his life — and nothing I can say or do will change that.

I exhale and go in search of the water I should have well and truly been back with by now.

By the time I get back to the table, Jackson is nowhere to be seen.

***

"I forgot how good carbs taste." Tillie groans in appreciation as she sucks the last of the flavouring off one of her fingers. "Those are definitely going on the menu."

"You've said that about every option so far," I say with a laugh.

"I'm not even sorry." She smirks. "And Reece isn't here to give his opinion, so we're just going to have to have them all I think."

She's much more emotionally stable with some decent food under her belt. Bryn might be a right pain in my ass, but I owe him for that at least.

And compared to the other extravagant requests I've had thrown my way, courtesy of Tillie, this is barely even a big deal.

"Where did lover boy go?" she asks as she looks around the room.

I shrug. "I'm not sure."

"You're falling for this guy, aren't you?" she asks, her tone serious.

Apparently, this is confess-your-feelings Thursday.

There's no point in hiding things from Tillie or changing the subject, she knows me well enough to know when I'm lying or trying to avoid talking about something.

"I'm falling hard, Tills, and even though I know he's not going to be there to catch me, I can't make it stop."

I wouldn't want to make it stop either, this is the path my life is taking — whether or not he joins me on this trail is still very much up for debate, but either way, it doesn't change the direction I'm heading.

"He might surprise you."

I shrug. "He might."

"And if he doesn't?" she asks.

"Then he doesn't."

"You're so *reasonable*." She says it like it's a foreign concept to her, because quite frankly, being reasonable isn't Tillie's specialty.

I laugh. "And that makes one of us."

I hear the door open again and I see Reece rushing through it.

"He's here," I tell her brightly.

She smiles instead of scowls so I figure it's safe to leave them alone.

"I'm going to go find Jackson and tell him you want it all, I'll see you tomorrow?"

"See you then."

"Get some of this to take away and eat it before I see you again. You're less scary when you're full."

"Oh, ha ha," she mocks as I walk away.

I give Reece a quick hello and a kiss on the cheek before heading off in search of Jackson.

One of the servers points me in the direction of Jackson's apartment so I climb the stairs and knock on the door.

I can't explain why, but I'm filled with nerves as I wait for him to answer.

I hear his footsteps as he approaches the door before the handle turns and it opens in front of me.

CHAPTER FIFTEEN

Jackson

I knew she wouldn't just leave without saying goodbye, yet when I open the door and she's standing there in front of me, somehow looking even more beautiful than she did half an hour ago, it still surprises me enough to render me speechless.

She smiles at me. "You disappeared."

I most certainly did.

After I saw her talking to Bryn I couldn't stomach being there anymore. I had to get the fuck out and try and make sense of my head.

I've never seen red like that in my life.

A surge of jealously raged through my body as I watched her looking up at him, taking over my blood stream and pumping envy through my veins.

It came from nowhere and caught me completely off guard.

What made it worse, was the fact that Tillie had a front-row seat to my moment of realisation.

"Look, I know that Katie is all about letting people figure things out for themselves and all that, but I'm more of a 'dude, what the fuck?' kinda girl — so news flash, she likes you. And I'm pretty sure you're into her too."

I stood there like an idiot, as I listened to someone else point out the way I'm feeling, because I *am* feeling.

I'm feeling a whole lot for the woman in front of me.

She frowns at me when I don't answer her. "Are you okay?"

"I'm good," I find myself saying, even though I feel anything but.

"Can I come in?"

I push the door open wider so she can walk through, but I make no effort to move out of her way.

Her arm brushes against mine as she walks by and the floral scent of her perfume fills my nose.

She doesn't sit like she normally would, instead she tosses her bag onto the couch and slides off her sandals, then she just stands there, looking at me.

She's such a beautiful woman, that I just stare right back at her.

"Are you going to tell me what's going on?" she asks after a few beats of silence.

"I saw you and Bryn," I blurt out before I've even had the chance to decide if I'm going to talk to her about this or not.

"You did, huh?" she asks. "And what exactly did you see?"

"He was close to you. Flirting with you."

"He was," she says.

"I didn't like it."

"I'll be sure to tell him it had the desired effect."

I frown at her in confusion as my brain tries to make sense of what she's saying and fails. My head is whirring, it's full of Lizzie and Bryn and Katie... and *more* Katie.

"He wanted to make you jealous, dreamboat, so that you'd realise you've got feelings for me."

He did fucking *what?*

"I'll be sure to tell him it had the desired effect," I mimic her words back to her in a whisper.

"I'm not going out with him, Jackson. I don't play those kinds of games," she says and I don't think she's heard what I said.

I take a couple of steps towards her. I don't even know what I'm doing anymore. I can keep telling myself that everything I've been doing isn't to try and impress her, but that won't change the fact that I *am*.

I'm thinking about her without even knowing I'm doing it.

I don't know what's going on with me, but I know one thing for certain. I want her. I need her... In some way *more* than what I have her now.

Tillie's words echo in my brain again as I take another couple of steps closer to Katie.

"I know she comes across as tough and sure of herself, but she's like a crème egg — hard exterior and all gooey in the centre — just be gentle with her."

The last thing I want to do is hurt Katie, but I can't deny myself any longer.

That kiss between us at the beach the other day was electric, and I want that again. I can't stop thinking about it — no matter how hard I've tried to forget it ever happened.

I've got a pretty good feeling she does too.

She could be downstairs agreeing to a date with my best mate, but she's not — she's here with me.

I reach for her face and cup it in my palm. She closes her eyes and leans into my touch.

"What's going on here, Katie?" I murmur as I look down at her.

Her eyes flutter open, and those dark eyes are staring at me again.

"I'm having a hard time thinking of something to say that won't scare you off," she confesses as she reaches up to wrap her arms around my neck.

"You couldn't scare me off."

"I can't give you no-strings," she says.

"I don't want no-strings," I promise as my arm snakes around her waist, bringing her closer to me.

"I don't want promises you can't keep."

"I'm not making any promises."

"Good," she breathes.

"Can we just agree that we'll see where this goes?"

She nods, her eyes still locked on mine.

"I lied. I want us to make one promise," I say before it's too late.

Her mouth is begging mine to meet it, and I know once that happens, I won't have the same restraint I had on the beach the other day.

"What?"

"I want you to promise that you'll tell me what you want."

"I promise."

I brush my lips against hers softly. "What do you want, dimples?" I whisper against her mouth.

"Right now, I just want *you*."

That's the easiest request I've ever heard.

I press my lips against hers and she clings on around my neck.

She moans softly as I grab hold of her ass and lift her into my arms.

I walk us towards the couch and lower her down.

She looks up at me as I lift her shirt over her head.

"Make me yours, Jackson," she whispers as she returns the favour and removes my shirt.

I intend to do exactly that.

I shudder as her long nails run over my skin.

This isn't at all like the first time, this is different. There are feelings other than lust involved this time. Bryn, Tillie, they're right — I'm feeling things for Katie, and I'm going to show her exactly what those feelings are, with my body.

***

"We'll make it to the bed next time, scouts honour," I promise her.

"I look forward to it."

She gratefully takes the glass of water I'm holding out for her and she sips the cool liquid.

I can't take my eyes off her; everything she does fascinates me. I know I'm smiling, and I don't even know why, it's just her — she makes me happy.

"I like you, dreamboat." She blurts out the words and her expression transforms into one of worry.

I smile a little wider. "I like you too, dimples," I reply, and her features relax again.

I don't have any idea where we'll go from here, or if I'm even capable of giving her all of me, but I'm not going to worry about that now. I'm more than content with 'like' at this stage.

"Good."

"If you give me half an hour, I might be able to show you just how much I like you all over again." I wink at her.

"And they say romance is dead."

I laugh low and long.

"I don't know what I did before you came along," I confess.

"Before you used to drink like a fish you mean?" she teases me.

I rest my knee on the couch next to her hip and hover above her, our chests touching lightly. "You're making everything glow again," I whisper.

She bites down on her lip as her eyes take in every bare inch of my body.

I know I said I needed half an hour, but I don't know who I was kidding. I want her again already.

I've resisted all of this for so long, but not anymore. Now I'm going to get my fill of her.

I lower myself down, and given the soft moan she makes, I know she's feeling the same way.

CHAPTER SIXTEEN

Katie

To: Katie
  From: Jackson

I miss you.

To: Jackson
  From: Katie

You miss me, or your penis misses me?

To: Katie
  From: Jackson

Would it be the wrong answer if I said we both do?

To: Jackson

From: Katie

I think it would be the honest answer, dreamboat.

To: Katie
    From: Jackson

Can me and my honest penis come over then?

To: Jackson
    From: Katie

I have to meet a new client in two hours, come over instead so we've got more time?

To: Katie
    From: Jackson

That's cute that you think I could last two hours. I'll see you in five.

I shake my head in amusement. It's been the same story every day for the past week.

He can't seem to get enough of me, and I'm anything but complaining.

I don't know what the two of us are, but I do know that Jackson hasn't mentioned his ex once since things changed between us, and I'm taking that as a sign that he's finally moving on from that part of his life.

I'd be lying if I didn't say I hope he'll be moving on with me.

The more time I spend with him, and more specifically *under* him, the harder I fall.

There hasn't been a period of time more than a few hours long in which I haven't heard from him. He calls and texts me so often I feel like I've become one of those girls who are constantly looking at their phone.

I feel giddy, happy and in love.

I'm *totally* in love with him.

There's no point trying to deny it, or hold back my feelings anymore. Something like this can't be denied.

I must have got caught up thinking about Jackson, because I'm startled by a knock at the door.

I scramble out of my chair and jog across the room. I can't get to him fast enough.

"Hey, beautiful," he says as I open the door, and I fall just a little bit deeper again. He's wearing that grin of his, the one that melts me.

I think he could get me to do anything he wanted if he smiled at me like that.

He chuckles at me and I blush.

"I think I missed you too," I whisper.

"I think I like the sound of that."

***

He pulls me back to him and kisses me again.

"I'm going to be late," I murmur against his lips.

I'm making no real move to leave either, but he's certainly not making it easy for me to walk away.

"So, go then," he says as he pulls away.

"I need to," I say as I drag him back against me.

His lips find mine again and I feel his tongue trace the curve of my bottom lip.

"I really have to go," I say, with all the willpower of a jelly-fish.

He chuckles and rests his forehead against mine.

"Call me when you're done?"

I nod.

"Come for dinner at my place."

I nod once more.

He kisses me again, one quick chaste kiss and then moves back.

I don't know how he does that. I'm a strong woman, but one kiss from him turns me to mush.

My head gets cloudy and the responsibilities of my world all fall away.

I shake my head in an attempt to clear it.

"I really have to go."

He leans against the door of his car and crosses his arms across his chest.

He looks like a god damn male model standing there like that, and it gives me goosebumps as I think about the fact that he's looking at *me*.

I climb into my car before my will power escapes me entirely and blow him a kiss as I drive away.

***

I arrive at my usual spot to meet clients and give Johnny, the owner, a wave.

Thanks to Jackson and his all-consuming energy, I am in fact running a few minutes late, so when I look over to my usual booth and see a lone male, I'm confused.

I approach the man and smile warmly at him. "Grant?" I ask.

He stands and smiles back at me. "You must be Katie."

I take the hand he's extended to me and shake it firmly.

He gestures for me to sit down and I do.

"Sorry, Elizabeth is running about ten minutes late, she should be here soon."

"No worries at all," I say as I pull my planner out of my bag and sit it on the table in front of me.

He picks up his cup of coffee and takes a sip.

Under normal circumstances, I would have thought that he was an extremely attractive man, but given that I can't shake Jackson and his smiling perfection from my mind, Grant isn't having quite the same effect.

I flip open my planner. "We can go over a few details while we wait anyway; you were planning a wedding for next summer, is that right?"

"Correct."

"Did you have a date in mind?"

"I think Elizabeth had a few possibilities written down." He chuckles, "I'm sorry, I won't be much help — there seems to be a lot of information I'm not privy to."

"Excellent." I smile at him. "You sound like a typical groom."

He holds his hands up. "Guilty."

"Have you decided on a location or will we need to go through some options?"

"I just know she wants it in a garden somewhere."

I nod as I scrawl that down on my page.

"I'm so sorry I'm late," a breathless voice says.

I smile as I look up from my page and then like a blow to the gut, the smile falls off my face.

I've seen this blonde woman who looks a lot like a Barbie doll before.

I glance down at her left hand and sure enough, it's the same bony fingers — only this time, it's a different rock.

I've literally come face to face with my worst nightmare.

"This is Elizabeth," Grant tells me, breaking me from my trance.

"All my friends call me Lizzie," she says as she holds her hand out to me.

I don't take her hand. I just stare at her, then at him, then at her again.

"Oh god, it's *you*."

"I'm sorry, do I know you?" she asks as she looks at her fiancé in confusion.

"No, no you don't." I shake my head rapidly. "We've never met."

"Um, you're not making any sense," she says.

I hold my face in my hands for a few seconds, willing this to all be a bad dream.

Of all the couples and all the wedding planners, fate had to match the two of us together.

It hits me then what that rock on her stupid hand means — she's getting married, and this man in front of me is probably *him*. He's most likely the man who stabbed Jackson in the back.

"I know who you are," I say, and I can hear the strength coming back to my voice.

The shock has worn off and been promptly replaced with anger.

I'm angry as hell with the two of them.

She giggles nervously and looks at Grant again. He shrugs at her.

"I'm a friend of Jackson's."

Her face visibly pales and her jaw falls slack. Grant's expression turns sheepish and I know then that he *is* the one.

"He's told me *all* about the two of you actually," I say as I shut the planner in front of me. I won't be needing it here — there's no way I'm planning this wedding now — not for all the money in the world.

I could get up and leave, but I'm not quite done here yet.

"He told me about how you slept with his best friend and ran out on him." I look at her as I speak before turning to him. "And he told me how you claimed the woman he was going to marry as your own, without so much as two fucks given about your so-called mate."

"We never meant to hurt him," Lizzie says, her voice barely above a whisper.

She looks like she's seen a ghost and I'd be lying if I said I wasn't enjoying her obvious discomfort.

"Really? That old chestnut?" I raise my brows at her. "You know what, *Lizzie*?" I sneer. "If you didn't want to hurt him, you could have *not* fucked his best mate. That would have been a good start."

Her eyes widen.

I'm not exactly being quiet, and some of the tables around us look like they're ready to bust out the popcorn and enjoy the show.

I grab my planner and begin stuffing it into my bag.

"Wait, where are you going?" she asks me in a panicked voice.

I huff out a laugh. "Lady, if you think I'm planning *your* wedding, you must be high. Unlike you, I have morals." I look her up and down as I get to my feet. "And class."

I take a couple of steps away but change my mind and go back.

"And one more thing... You traded *Jackson* for him? Girl, get your eyes checked."

I give Grant one last look and word of advice. "If she'll do it *with* you, she'll do it *to* you, just sayin'." I smirk at him before I turn on my heel and stalk out of the café.

I hope my performance came across more confident than I feel right now, I'm literally trembling.

I've just made one hell of a scene at my usual spot, but that's not even what's got me shaken as I get into my car and start the engine. My biggest concern is that I'm going to have to break it to Jackson that the two people who hurt him the most are living happily ever after, *together*.

CHAPTER SEVENTEEN

Jackson

My phone rings on my desk and I smile before I've even picked it up.

This whole thing with Katie is going better than I could have imagined. She's everything I've ever wanted in a woman, combined with all the things I never would have thought to ask for.

It sounds cheesy and cliché, but she's perfect — for me at least.

She makes me forget all the bullshit in my past, and I'm finally getting to a point where I'm spending more time looking forward than I am looking back.

I tap the green icon to answer her call. "I was just thinking about you."

"Jackson," she says, and I can immediately tell something's up. She's shaken.

"Dimples, are you okay?"

I get up from my chair and shut the door to my office.

"I'm okay... I mean, I'm *not* okay, but I'm not hurt or anything." She exhales deeply, and I can hear an actual tremor in her breathing.

"What's going on?" I demand. If someone has done something to upset her, they're going to have me to deal with.

She sucks in a deep breath and blows it out again before finally speaking.

"You know how I said I had a client I had to meet after I left you?"

"Yeah..."

There's silence for long enough to make me nervous before she finally speaks again.

"It was Lizzie... and Grant."

"*Lizzie and Grant*? But you're a wedding planner..." It's as I'm saying the words that I realise exactly what that means.

They're getting *married*.

My ex is getting married... to someone who I once considered a friend.

"I'm so sorry, Jackson," she whispers. "I swear I didn't know it was going to be them. You never told me what his name was, and she contacted me as Elizabeth... I didn't know."

Of course she didn't know. She never would have met with them if she did.

"What happened?" I demand in a tone far harsher than I intended.

"I walked out," she tells me quietly. "I *might* have said some things to her..."

"Might have?"

"Okay I *definitely* said some things — to both of them, but I couldn't get out of there fast enough if I'm completely honest."

"So, you're not planning their wedding?"

She huffs out a laugh. "Hell freakin' no. Are you insane?"

I nod my head even though she can't see me. "Good," I growl. "And yeah... Maybe."

I'm pacing the room, I don't know what to do with myself. I'm torn between screaming or punching something, but I can't do either of those things with Katie on the phone.

None of this is her fault, but my carefully constructed, content little world has just come crashing down around me all over again.

This isn't two steps forward and one step backwards, this is more like two steps forward and then a flat-out sprint in the opposite direction.

Right now, I'm back in the kitchen with Lizzie and she's telling me that she met someone else. That she's leaving. That we're over.

I'm right back to having my heart broken.

"Are you okay?" Katie asks, and honestly, I'd forgotten she was still there, on the other end of the phone that's pressed to my ear.

I can't let her see this — the meltdown I can feel brewing. I've already put her through so much and given her so little in return, I don't want her to see me like this.

"Can we take a rain check on dinner tonight?" I manage to choke out. "I won't be very good company."

"Jackson... *Please* don't do this," she begs.

She knows me well enough to know what's going on right now — she knows I'm close to the point of falling apart.

"I'm fine," I tell her, and it's a blatant lie — the first outright lie I've ever told her, and I hate myself for it the minute I say it.

I'm not fine at all. She knows it as well as I do, and I can feel myself pushing her away when I know I should be holding her close, but I'm all fucked up.

She's quiet for a long time and when she does speak it threatens to break my heart even more than Lizzie ever could.

"I really care about you, Jackson. I'm here if you need me, okay? Just pick up the phone and call me. I promise I won't let you down... I'm not her."

I don't even get a chance to reply before the line goes dead.

I squeeze the phone in my hand and consider throwing it against the wall of my office, but I don't. Even in my all-consuming rage, I can hear Katie's words echoing in my head over and over again, telling me to pick up the phone and call her.

She's always the voice of reason.

I won't call her back — not while I'm in this frame of mind, but something inside my brain tells me that I shouldn't eliminate the option entirely. I don't want to let her down any more than I already have.

I settle for slamming it down on the couch and letting out a frustrated half scream.

I need a fucking drink.

I think I need about ten drinks actually and lucky for me, I'm in the right place.

***

"You know... it's just *bullshit*... ya know?" I look around blindly, trying to find where I left Bryn.

"Right here, big guy," he tells me as he sits down next to me and claps me on the shoulder. "And I hear ya, it's bullshit."

"Bullshit," I mutter under my breath as I take another swig of my drink.

"This is going to sound like a cliché, but you know you're better off without her, right? Let Grant have your sloppy leftovers."

I glare at him and toss back another shot of I don't even know what.

"That doesn't make me feel any better."

"Well it should. Lizzie was a bitch."

"Bitch," I mumble in agreement.

I gesture Nick to come over and refill me, but Bryn warns him off with a wave of his hand. "You're done here, boss man."

"But this is my bar," I slur.

Even I know I'm too pissed, but like a true drunken asshole, I'm not willing to go quietly. I'm like my own worst nightmare on a bar shift right now.

"You're damn right it's yours, and you've got a shit load of paying customers in here, so how about you stop threatening to make a scene and go up to bed quietly instead."

I try to spin on my seat so I'm looking at him, but I somehow manage to end up falling to the floor.

"Ouch," Bryn drawls. "The floor's a really good look on you, boss."

"I'll give you ouch in a minute," I say as I try and get to my feet and fail miserably.

"Oh yeah, you're a real Rocky right now." He chuckles as he helps me up and steadies me.

"Just give me a bottle and I'll be on my way," I barter with him.

"You'll be on your way *without* a bottle," he tells me. He's not buying into my bullshit one little bit.

He's leading me to the stairs, and I laugh to myself as I recall flashes of Katie trying to help me do this same thing.

"I *really* have to stop drinking this time," I think aloud.

"Understatement of the fucking century, dude." He grunts. "Shit, can you help me out at all here? You're a god damn dead weight."

I grin lazily at him as he struggles to help me up the stairs. He's panting like a big dog. "Too much weights, not enough cardio," I tell him, matter of factly. "You've gotta start going for runs, man... clears the... head," I tell him as I tap my skull.

"Right... because your head seems so fucking clear."

He shoves me so I'm leaning against the wall next to my door as he rests his hands on his knees and breathes hard.

"In you fucking go." He points at the door.

I pull my keys out of my pocket and look at them in confusion. They all look a little blurry, and shiny, and most confusing of all, they all look the same.

"Oh, for the love of God," he huffs as he snatches them from my hand and finds the key without much effort at all.

"How'd you do that?" I ask as he opens the door and shoves me inside before following me in.

"I'm going back downstairs to close up. You — go to bed."

I salute him as I stumble inside.

"I fucking mean it, Jack, just go to sleep, alright? Don't make any phone calls or any of that shit, you'll just make a fool of yourself."

"Sleep. No calls," I repeat back to him.

He shakes his head at me and strides across the room to the door.

"Love you, B," I yell after him.

He turns and laughs at me as he pulls the door shut.

I look around the empty apartment and frown.

I manage, with a lot of freaking effort, to toe off my shoes and flop down on the couch.

I want to call Katie, but first I need to shut my eyes for a few minutes, I decide as I feel my lids growing heavy before they close altogether.

CHAPTER EIGHTEEN

Katie

He hasn't called me. Not even one damn phone call.

It's been *hours*, and if I know him as well as I think I do, he'll be well and truly wasted by now.

Drowning his sorrows yet again.

The man is so emotionally damaged and the only kind of coping method he has is one you find at the bottom of a bottle.

My life feels like it's all coming to a point where it's all going to explode. The lease on my apartment is up in a month, Tillie's wedding is in three weeks, and I'm in love with a man who is still obsessing over his breakup with his ex.

All these things, they're coming to a head — I can feel it. As much as I love my best friend and want her to be happy and have a beautiful day, I absolutely can't wait for her wedding to be over.

I need some air.

That's why I came out here, to the beach he brought me too. But it's not giving me the same sense of peace that it did when he was here with me.

It's not the same without him.

Out here now I just feel lonely and confused, and neither of those emotions are something I'm particularly accustomed to feeling.

It's funny how finding someone you want to share your life with can make you feel whole yet empty at the same time.

I don't like it — this feeling of giving up control and putting my fate into the hands of someone else.

I know Jackson feels things for me — these past couple of weeks have been the most incredible weeks of my life, but like my dad always used to say, 'what goes up, must come down', and I've got a pretty good idea that the 'coming down' is happening right now.

I brush the sand off my hands and get to my feet. It's nearly pitch black out here, and it's freezing.

It's time for me to go.

Where I'm going, I have no idea... But I know I can't sit here static forever. Whatever is going to happen in my life requires me to be *in* it; I just have to ride it out and see where it takes me.

CHAPTER NINETEEN

Jackson

I wake with a start and realise it's my own snoring that has dragged me from my drunken slumber.

I blink a few times against the harsh ceiling lights.

"What the fuck," I mutter to myself as I sit up and run my hand through my hair.

I'm still wasted. I can feel the alcohol thrumming through my veins.

I'm home at least, and alone by the looks, so those are both wins.

But my ex-girlfriend and mate are getting hitched, and that certainly isn't a win.

I pick up my phone and stare at the screen as I think about what to do next.

The more rational part of my brain is telling me to hit the hay and call it a night, but the little devil that sits on my shoulder — the one who seems to get bigger and louder every time I drink — is telling me that I'm still pissed off and I need to do something about it.

I slide open the screen of my phone and dial the number I have saved for the cab company.

I don't even realise exactly what I'm doing until I'm giving them my address for pickup and telling them where I want to go.

I know it's a bad idea, I *do*, and if someone was here to save me from myself right now, I'd be fucking grateful, but there's not.

There's just me, the silence and my pathetic wounded heart.

I manage to get my shoes back on my feet and before I know it, I'm down the stairs — the exterior ones, I can't risk Bryn intercepting me — and into the waiting cab.

I must be drunker than I thought, because I swear I blink and we're there — outside the house that is all too familiar to me.

"Keep the meter running," I say with a point of my finger. "Got it? I just gotta say a couple things and I'll be back... Keep the meter running." I shake my head at myself. "I said that already."

"I'll be waiting," the driver tells me.

I think he wants me out of his car, but after I clamber out and walk up the path, I look back and he's still there.

I give him a double thumbs up and he gives me an awkward one back.

I approach the door and knock hard.

I'm not expecting her to actually be here, so when the door opens inwards and she's standing there in front of me, I say her name aloud like I'm shocked to see her here — at the place where she lives.

"Jackson?" Lizzie asks in confusion. "What are you doing here?"

"I used to live here, you know," I say as I sway a little bit. "Why are *you* here?"

"Are you *drunk*?" she asks, her voice rising an octave.

I look her up and down out of habit — she's a beautiful woman, but there's something wrong, she still looks the same, all tall, blonde and skinny, but there's something missing. She just looks *wrong* — that's the only way I can explain it.

"I might have had a couple. Katie says I need to stop drinking."

"I think you should listen to Katie," she says as she looks anxiously up and down the street.

"I *should*." I agree with a vigorous nod. "She's a smart woman."

"Why are you here, Jackson?"

"You're getting married." I don't say it like a question, I throw it at her like an accusation.

She blushes deep red and dips her chin in embarrassment.

"Katie told me," I add.

"Did she tell you she yelled at me?"

I shrug.

"I guess I deserved it," she says, and even drunk, I'm surprised she's admitting to deserving anything other than a happy ever after.

I stuff my hands in my pockets and try to stop swaying from side to side.

I think I fail.

"Katie says I need to stop being mad at you."

"You're *still* mad at me?" she asks, and if I didn't know better, I would have sworn that this information hurt her in some way.

I must really be drunk — Lizzie doesn't get hurt. She only does the hurting.

"Really fucking mad," I say.

"Grant and I—"

"*Grant and I*," I interrupt her with a poorly done impression of her voice.

She winces.

"I don't give a *fuck* about you and Grant," I say, a slur creeping into my voice.

"Then why *are* you here?" she asks me gently.

I shrug again.

Truthfully, I don't really know why I'm here. I thought I cared about her still, I really did, but standing here in front of her, I feel *nothing*. She's the wrong woman.

"I'm really sorry that I hurt you, Jackson, I *am*, and I know that my opinion doesn't count for anything anymore, but I think you need to open your eyes and see this Katie woman. Really *see* her. Because it seems to me that she's telling you all the right things, and judging by the way she stood up for you today, it looks like she's doing all the right things too. She's in love with you, Jackson, and the way you say her name makes me think you could fall in love with her too."

"I'm already in love with her," I snap at her, and the words shock me so much I look around to check that it was me that said them.

"Well... shit," I mutter. It's like someone just opened a door inside my brain, or maybe being here and letting go of all this bullshit unlocked it for me and shoved me through to the other side.

I don't know what was holding me back before, whether it was fear or something else, but now that those words have left my mouth and found their way out into the universe, it seems like the most obvious thing in the world.

I *love* her.

I'm in love with Katie, and I'm ruining it. I'm screwing the whole thing up.

"Go home, Jackson," Lizzie says, and I snap my eyes back up to her face.

"Maybe I will," I say — totally unwilling to admit that maybe she might be right.

I can feel the slur growing thicker in my voice. I *should* get the hell out of here.

"I really am sorry, Jackson. I know there's nothing I can say, but I do hope you'll be happy one day."

I'll be happy sooner than one day. I'm already happy, I just didn't know it.

"Good talk," I say as I turn around and make my way down the path. "I still really don't fucking like you, but good talk," I yell over my shoulder.

I climb into the cab without so much as a backwards glance.

"Back home?" the driver asks me hopefully.

I shake my head at him. "Nope. I *love* her."

"So, you're getting back out then?" he asks in confusion as he looks up at the house.

"Not *her*," I say with a scowl. "Just drive, man, I'll tell you the way."

He mutters something under his breath that sounds suspiciously like 'drunk ass' before taking off down the street.

CHAPTER TWENTY

Katie

"Katie!" I hear the voice yell. "Katie? Are you there?"

I rush over to the monitor on the wall and listen to make sure I'm not hearing things.

"Katie! Open up, dimples," he yells again.

"Jesus Christ," I mutter.

It's late... or early, depending on which way you look at it, and Jackson is loud as all hell.

I press the button so I can talk back to him. "Jackson?" I ask.

"The one and only," he drawls, and I can hear that he's been drinking.

"What are you doing here?"

"I need to come up," he says in a voice so loud I have to move my ear away from the speaker.

"You're drunk as hell, can you *please* keep it down?"

"Lemme up."

I close my eyes and deliberate for a minute.

On the one hand, he's *here*, when he could be god knows where else instead, but on the other hand, he's drunk — *again*.

"I caaaan't stop, and I wooooon't stop." He starts singing Miley at the top of his lungs, and I slam my hand on the button to open the door for him before he can wake up the entire neighbourhood.

"Sweet Jesus... Be quiet on your way up," I hiss at him.

I cover my face with my hands and groan. I don't know what I'm doing, or what I'm hoping for, one thing I do know is that him turning up in the middle of the night when he's been on the turps is probably not a good thing.

I hear a noise at the door that sounds a lot like a single finger tapping lightly against the wood.

"Good luck to me," I mumble as I open the door.

He's leaning against the door frame and he wobbles a little bit as the door moves.

"*Katie*," Jackson says, and the way it comes out sounds like pure relief. "I'm so happy you're home."

"Shhhh," I hiss as I grab his arm and drag him inside. "You're seriously the loudest human in the world."

"Do you really think I'm the loudest?" He looks at me with wide eyes. "Should we call the record books?"

I can't help but laugh. He's *so* drunk, but so funny.

"Let's save the phone calls for the morning, yeah?"

"You're so smart, dimples," he says as he lets me lead him to the couch.

"How'd you get here?"

"Cab. I sent him home though. He was getting sick of my shit."

"I can't imagine why." I giggle as he lands his butt on the couch with a thud.

He closes his eyes and leans his head back against the cushion. "I just need to close my eyes for a little minute and then I wanna talk to you."

I reach for a blanket on the arm of the couch and drape it over him. He won't last another thirty seconds.

Whatever big talking plans he's got — they'll have to wait until morning.

"Dimples?" he says with a yawn.

"Yeah, dreamboat?"

"Lizzie was right, I *should* listen to you."

I stare at him, unsure of what to say, not that it would matter anyway — he's softly snoring now.

'Lizzie was right'... I don't know what that means, but my gut tells me it can't be good.

I sit next to him on the couch and tug half his blanket over me. I was bone tired before he turned up here, but I doubt I'll sleep a wink now.

I know I'm stupid for getting attached to a man who isn't emotionally available, but it didn't seem like I had a choice.

I guess this is the part where I have to accept that whatever will be, will be. It's what I've thought I believed my entire life, but now that I'm here, in love with the most incredible man I've ever met, I really want him to love me back. I don't want to hear him mention his ex's name as he falls asleep.

I want him to be saying mine.

That's the universe for you though, it's got a mind of its own.

I sigh as I lay my head back and close my eyes. I beg for sleep to take me, but I know it probably won't.

I listen to each inhale and exhale of his breath and hope that tomorrow he'll wake up and it'll be my name he says.

***

"Wake up, dimples," I hear Jackson whisper.

I smile at the sound of his voice, even half asleep he still makes me smile.

"Five more minutes," I answer sleepily.

I don't know when I finally drifted off, but I feel like I've only had about thirty minutes sleep.

I'm shattered.

I spent all night thinking about Jackson and me, and what the hell we're going to do.

"You can sleep when you're dead." He chuckles as he tries to pry my arms from my face.

"You and your snoring didn't get that memo last night," I grumble.

He snuggles his face into the crook of my neck and kisses me, just one soft kiss. "I'm sorry if I kept you up all night."

I breathe in his scent. He smells like whiskey and fast food.

"You smell," I murmur as he sits back up. "Like alcohol and shit food."

I don't know how he does it, fresh from sleep and no doubt sporting a hangover, he still looks sexy as hell — even if he doesn't smell so great.

"I had a *great* pie last night." He holds out the hem of his shirt and looks down it, presumably to see if he lost any down the front, and judging by the stain halfway down, he did.

"Oh, I bet it was the best pie you've *ever* tasted," I say with a roll of my eyes.

"How'd you know?" He chuckles with a wink.

I almost sigh as I watch him smile at me. I don't want to give him up. I don't want to only be his friend.

"So, you went on another drinking bender..." I prompt.

He shoots me a sheepish look. "I seem to have a habit of drowning my sorrows at the bottom of a bottle."

I nod. Can't argue with the truth.

He fidgets nervously with the blanket I threw over us last night. And I can tell he's got something more to say — whatever it was that he came here to tell me is about to come out.

"It happened again," he says. "I went to see Lizzie."

I knew this was coming, truly I did, yet I still feel the force of his words hitting me like a punch to the chest.

"She was home this time," he carries on.

My heart rate has risen to a gallop, and nothing I can tell myself seems to be able to slow it down.

"And how did that go for you?" I manage to ask.

"It went well actually, *really* well." His voice sounds serene, like he's finally found peace, and with every word he speaks, my heart sinks a little further into my stomach.

"I'm happy for you," I whisper, and suddenly I can't be here a minute longer; I feel physically sick, like I might throw up.

I don't know what I was thinking, telling Lizzie that she was stupid to choose Grant over Jackson. I practically put the idea of taking him back into her head.

"I'm *sorry*," I say as I jump to my feet and attempt to bolt to my bedroom, but he's too fast. He's on his feet in a flash and catches my arm, pulling me to a halt.

"Dimples, what's wrong?" he asks, his handsome face a mask of concern. "Why are you running?"

"I want you to be happy, Jackson, I do, but I can't watch you go back to her, not when I love you the way that I do."

The corners of his mouth turn up slowly, until a full smile graces his face.

"I knew you'd fall in love with me. I told you that you would."

I sniff back the tears that are threatening to fall and pull my arm from his grasp. "Well congratulations, you were right after all. Are you happy now?"

I turn away from him and head for my room again so he can't see the hurt in my eyes, but it feels wrong. I hate this version of myself. I'm okay with being vulnerable, but I don't know how to deal with *this*.

Being in love hurts.

"Katie," he says and his voice stops me in my tracks.

I feel him come up behind me, he's standing so close I can feel the heat of his body through my clothes.

"I'm not going back to *her*, not in a million damn years."

I hear his words, but they can't be right. He's still all messed up over her. He goes back to her constantly without even knowing he's doing it.

I turn slowly around so I'm facing him. "You're not?"

He shakes his head and runs his hand down my arm. "Not when I love you the way I do," he says, mimicking my earlier sentiments.

I can almost feel my heart catapult from my stomach back up into my chest where it belongs.

The sick feeling disappears as his eyes search mine, saying everything I've ever wanted to hear from him without actually saying any words at all.

"You're finally over her?" I ask in a whisper.

I want to believe it could be true, but I won't until I hear the words from him.

"I stood in front of her and felt *nothing*," he says in a voice that is so honest I'd never doubt it. "All I could think about was *you*. I've been over her ever since I met you — I just didn't know it."

"You love me?"

"I think I've loved you a long time, dimples, I've just been stupid and blind."

"I've loved you a long time too," I confess.

"You didn't tell me."

"I knew you weren't ready to hear it."

He shakes his head in disbelief.

"You are the most patient woman in the whole world," he says as he wraps his arms around my waist and drags me against him.

"Tell me about it," I say with a roll of my eyes. "But some things are worth waiting for."

CHAPTER TWENTY-ONE

Jackson

I lean down and kiss her, and every inch of my body is over-come with a feeling of relief.

This is where I'm meant to be.

She pulls back and grips my chin between her thumb and finger. "I mean this in the nicest way possible, but you need a shower... and to brush your teeth."

I chuckle. "You're telling me that whiskey and pie isn't a winning flavour combination?"

"As tempting as it sounds, I'll take peppermint."

"Will you come home with me?" I ask as I brush the hair from her eyes. "I'll get less stinky, and you can get less clothed while you wait."

She rolls her eyes at me. "With pick-up lines of that calibre, how's a girl meant to resist?"

I chuckle. "I'll have to practice some new material on you."

"I think you've already successfully picked me up," she says, and I can hear the emotion in her voice. She really does love me.

"Let me grab some stuff." She goes to walk away, but I grab her hand, halting her.

"Pack a bag." I almost growl the words at her. "I'm not go-ing to let you out of my sight for a while."

"You kidnapping me, dreamboat?" she almost coos as she looks up at me.

"You'll have Stockholm syndrome by the time I'm finished with you."

She throws back her head and laughs, and it makes me so happy. "You are so strange."

"I love you, dimples."

"So you keep telling me." She smirks, all sass and smart mouth as she pulls away.

I smack her ass and send her off in the direction of her bedroom, but she simply turns and walks backwards slowly while her eyes stay trained on me.

"Any weird little quirks you want to share with me before I commit to doing this thing with you?" she asks, her tone teasing.

"There is *something*." I smirk. "I'm a closet Harry Potter fan."

She gasps. "*No!*"

"*Yes*." I chuckle.

"Wizards and shit?"

"My favourite character is Dobby."

She groans. "What the hell is a Dobby?"

"Surely you've heard of Dobby?" I ask as I flop down on her couch.

She lingers in the doorway. "I've heard of *Harry*. And what was that ginger kid's name, Rob? It's Rob, right?"

I shake my head in disappointment. "I might have to rethink having a relationship with you after this."

"Hey," she raises her hands in surrender, "you're a grown-ass man that likes movies about wizards, and *I'm* the disappointment here?"

I groan. "Please tell me that you're aware they were books before movies?"

She shrugs at me. "I'm more of a film kinda girl."

"Oh I know you are, I've seen your Netflix suggestions... You're the one who should be embarrassed out of the two of us."

She laughs and shakes her head at me. "If you say so, dreamboat."

"Go and pack your shit already, before I decide we have nothing in common." I grin at her.

"If only I owned a magic wand or some underwear with lightning bolts or something," she mocks me as she disappears from sight.

***

"Who the fuck cuts onions like that? I mean, *dude*! Are you serious? You just slice them... Oh for fuck's sake, give it here, I'll do it myself. Go and peel the potatoes. Surely you can't get that wrong."

Katie covers her mouth and giggles.

I shake my head in amusement. I don't know which one of my staff Bryn is yelling at this time, but he's been watching too much Gordon Ramsey by the sounds.

"Watch your language in front of my girlfriend," I tell him as I lead Katie into the kitchen by our joined hands.

I get a long, loud wolf whistle, courtesy of my best friend as a reply.

"Your *girlfriend,* you reckon?" Katie asks with one of her brows raised at me.

"Yeah. *Girlfriend.*" I grin at her. "If you'd had a wand or a wizard hat or something, I might have promoted you straight to fiancée."

"You're an asshole," she says as she smacks me on the arm.

"So, you finally listened to me, huh?" Bryn says smugly as he looks back and forth between the two of us.

I raise my brows at him in question.

"You went to bed and didn't do anything stupid last night," he prompts.

I shoot him a sheepish look.

Of course I didn't do that. That would have been the smart option, and if I've established one thing over the past twenty-four hours, it's that I do things the hard way whenever and wherever possible.

Katie snorts. "Oh no, he did *all* the stupid things. Then turned up on my door step smelling like grease and booze with something super important to say... Then he fell asleep."

"Oh man, c'mon!" He throws his hands in the air. "I gave you one instruction, Jack, *one*, and you say *I'm* the one who never listens."

"Yeah, yeah, get to the good bit already." I give her a gesture to wrap it up.

"Oh, you mean the part when you woke up and had figured out that you can't live without me?" She scrunches up her nose and grins at me.

I shrug at Bryn. "Who knew? Turns out I love her."

"I *knew* you liked that girl," he says as he raises his hand in the air. "I fucking knew it — you're a shitty liar."

I glance around the room, and everyone else in the kitchen has their hands raised too. "I think we all knew, boss," one of them calls out.

"Just me out of the loop then?" I look between them all. "Good. Excellent. That's just great."

"If it makes you feel any better, I think I might be in love with her too," Bryn tells me as he makes heart eyes at my girl.

That's when I know I'm finally over what happened with Lizzie — when a joke about my mate and my girlfriend makes me grin instead of wince.

"Get back to work before I cut you with your own knives," I threaten half-heartedly.

"*Feisty.*" He chuckles. "Calm yourself, Casanova, it's actually perfect that you're here — both of you." He looks at Katie. "That nightmare you call a best friend is coming in tonight to 'confirm the menu.'" He does a scarily accurate impression of Tillie's voice.

"Oh lord, that woman!" Katie groans. "We've confirmed the menu already."

Bryn shrugs. "I think she's just looking for a free feed from the hottest chef in town." He winks.

"I'll handle it," I tell Katie, who is now wrestling her cell phone out of her jeans pocket.

"I'll handle her just fine myself, thank you very much." She pulls the phone out finally and holds it up triumphantly.

I snag it out of her hands before she has the chance to verbally abuse her best friend.

"*I* will handle it, dimples."

She makes a humph noise and glares at me. "But it'll make me feel better to yell at her."

"That might be true, but I'm your boyfriend now, so it's my job to make sure you don't blow a gasket."

She pouts.

I take her hand and tow her out of the kitchen. "Clay!" I call.

He appears after a few seconds.

"I need a table for four tonight please."

He nods at me and disappears again.

"I've had sweet fuck-all sleep, dreamboat, I might kill her."

I wrap my arms around her and breathe in the scent of her perfume. "I'll make sure you can't reach the knives."

"You promise?"

I kiss the top of her head. "If I've managed this long without stabbing Bryn, the least you can do is not kill Tillie when she's only weeks away from being married. Imagine the news headlines."

"You're right," she says into the front of my shirt where she's buried her face. "Murdered bride-to-be doesn't read well."

"Especially when the bridesmaid did it," I chip in.

She sighs and looks up at me with her big dark eyes. "I've got something to ask you."

"I'm not killing her for you if that's where you're going with this." I chuckle. "I'm too pretty for prison."

She swats at my chest. "Not *that*. I wanted to ask you to be my plus one to the wedding."

"You're inviting me to the wedding from hell?"

"Bite your tongue, the wedding will be flawless — covered in flowers — but *flawless*, it's just the bride you've got to look out for... and if she doesn't calm down by then I'll have you spike her drink with a sedative anyway... so, problem solved."

"You're crazy."

"And *you're* coming with me to the wedding."

I cup her face in my hands and lean in to brush my lips against hers softly. "Maybe I could make an appearance, since I own the place and all."

She pushes up to her tip toes, and her lips graze my ear, making me shudder. "I'll make it worth your while," she whispers.

I don't know how she does that. I had her in the shower upstairs no more than an hour ago, but just like that I'm ready to go again.

If her best friend and this damn wedding doesn't turn out to be the death of me, then I think this woman just might finish the job herself.

CHAPTER TWENTY-TWO

Katie

"If she pushes my buttons tonight, I swear I'll slap her," I grumble as I pull out my chair at the table Jackson arranged for us.

I'm exhausted, thanks to the gorgeous man next to me. Frankly, he's lucky he's so god damn sweet and good looking right now because I'm not one of those people who can deal with getting no sleep. I'm a seven hours kind of girl. Five or six at an absolute push.

"I'll push your buttons later," Jackson tells me with a wink.

He waits for his lame joke to do its job and make me laugh, and it does.

It's really hard not to smile and laugh with him around. I hope that never changes between us.

"The eagle has landed," he whispers in my ear as he wraps his arm around me and pulls me in close.

"Well this looks awfully cosy." Tillie beams down at us as she and Reece reach the table hand in hand.

Jackson chuckles. "Have you met my girlfriend? She's extremely tired and she's also entirely out of fucks."

"Ohhh girrrrl," Tillie cries as I roll my eyes at Jackson. "It's about time you two got your shit together."

"The shit is officially together," Jackson announces as they take their seats.

"I'm happy for you, boo," Tillie says.

"I'm happy for me too, but seriously, what on earth do you need to check the menu for, yet again?" I whine at my best friend.

She smirks and darts her eyes between Jackson and me. "Huh. Colour me impressed, I thought you would have caved and told her," she says to Jackson. "You're such a pussy where she's concerned."

I frown at her and then at him. "Tell me what?"

Jackson grins at me triumphantly. "This isn't about the wedding. It's about *you*."

"Me?" I ask in surprise. "What? *Why?*"

Tillie reaches across the table and takes one of my hands in hers. "I wanted to thank you for putting up with all my shit. I'm a 'grade A' sociopath and you've dealt with it pretty well... You haven't had a go at killing me yet anyway."

"Debatable," I mutter under my breath.

Jackson takes my other hand. "And even though all I did was keep the secret, I'm going to jump in and take some credit, and thank you for putting up with all *my* shit too. You really are too good for me."

"For both of us," Tillie corrects him.

I can't believe she did this for me. And that she roped Jackson in and got this whole thing planned for me.

I almost feel bad for wanting to yell at her and possibly even stab her, but then I remember that I still have a couple more weeks of planning her wedding to go and I don't feel so guilty anymore. She'll drive me to the brink of insanity again before we get this thing done.

Tillie nudges Reece and gestures her head towards my hands.

He shrugs at her and she gives him a hard glare.

He lays his hand over top of Tillie's and mine. "I didn't know I had to prepare a speech, but how about I just promise you that you'll never have to plan another wedding for her?"

I giggle. "That would be great. You guys are so sweet," I say as I feel tears pooling in my eyes.

"Oh lord." Tillie groans as they let me go so I can wipe at my eyes. "You always get so teary when you're tired."

"Crying women make me nervous," Reece says as he eyes me anxiously.

I burst out laughing at his obvious discomfort. "You're lucky you've got the ice queen for a wife then, you won't have to worry about any of that with her."

"Hey! I cry on the inside." Tillie grins. "In a pretty, composed kind of way that doesn't involve my makeup getting messed up."

I laugh at her and dab at the liquid in the corners of my eyes. "But seriously, thank you for doing this, I really appreciate it."

"It's the least we could do."

"The least you could do is dial back the crazy, but since we both know that's a long shot, this will be sufficient."

"You know her so well," Reece teases as he looks at his wife-to-be with amusement.

"That she does," she agrees as she picks up the cocktail menu. "And since that works both ways... I know she needs one of those pretty pink drinks with the strawberries in it."

"I *do* need one of those." I nod in agreement.

Tillie stares at Jackson expectantly.

He chuckles. "Alright, I'm on it."

He kisses my temple again before sliding out of his seat.

***

"Do you want to go and look at apartments with me tomorrow? My lease is up just after your wedding and I'm not really liking the idea of being homeless."

"Oh no, sweetie, living under a bridge wouldn't be a good look for you."

I shake my head in amusement.

"Oooh! There's one just up the street from us that would be perfect for you." Tillie claps her hands together excitedly. "We could be neighbours."

"What are you jumping up and down about?" Jackson asks, his tone amused, as he slides back into his spot next to me.

"I'm going to show Katie the *best* apartment for her to lease," Tillie tells him excitedly.

He chuckles and shakes his head. "No need. I already found her a place."

I look at him in confusion. "You did?"

"Well this place is newly renovated," Tillie tells him, her tone sounding pissed that he's trying to mess with her new plan.

"Well this place has a view," Jackson argues.

"A park across the road."

"The beach at your fingertips."

"Me as a neighbour," Tillie argues, her expression turning triumphant, as though she's finally found the winning answer.

"Me as a roommate," Jackson replies softly, as he turns to face me.

"Huh?" I ask, totally shocked. I don't know what the hell just happened here, but this situation seems to have escalated rather quickly.

"I was going to ask you in private, but she egged me on," he explains.

I look over at Tillie and she's got one hand clapped over her mouth and the other shaking Reece's arm relentlessly to make sure he's paying attention to what's going down.

I turn my focus back to the man in front of me. "Are you asking me to move in here with you?"

He shrugs. "Yeah... I mean, why the hell not?"

"We only just became official," I breathe.

He shrugs again. "We go way back," he says with a cheeky grin. "May as well jump in head first, right?"

It's crazy, but I can't imagine saying no. I know how easily I could fall into a life with this man, even though he drives me insane half the time, there's nowhere else I'd rather be.

"Let's do it." I nod eagerly.

It takes a few seconds for my words to sink in, but when they do, the biggest smile graces his face. It's my favourite one.

"Sorry, Tills, but he beat you fair and square."

"Whoop!" Tillie exclaims. "Moving-in time, bitches!"

Jackson grabs hold of me and tugs me against his body. He plants a kiss to my temple before letting me go again.

I giggle gleefully.

"I think you and your ten-second relationship might be rubbing off on me," I tell Tillie with a roll of my eyes.

"As long as you wait until *after* my wedding to get engaged, mmkay?" She looks between the two of us pointedly.

"I think I can manage to wait another couple of weeks," Jackson jokes.

"I'm not sure how I'll cope that long without a ring on my finger, but you're the boss," I add sarcastically.

She nudges Reece. "Did you see that? My little girl is all grown up," she announces dramatically.

Jackson's hand finds mine under the table and he gives it a squeeze.

I grin at him and I know damn well that I may as well have hearts in my eyes.

I might still have one hell of a wedding to pull off, a house to move and whatever else this month decides to throw at me, but somehow, I've never felt more at ease in my whole life.

CHAPTER TWENTY-THREE

Jackson
Two weeks later

"These ones, dimples?" I ask, my voice strained under the weight of what I'm carrying.

She points to the furthest corner of the room and I grunt in response. I don't know what's in these boxes I'm lugging around, but they're heavy as fuck.

There's an entire team of people taking over my restaurant right now. They've only been in here a little over an hour, and I almost don't recognise the place already.

There's white, girly crap *everywhere*.

It's three in the morning and I'm not sure how much more of this I can handle before I have to excuse myself and hit the hay.

Tomorrow, technically *today*, is the big day, and Katie is in full-swing wedding-planner mode.

I'm impressed if not a little intimidated. She might be the sweetest, most kind-hearted woman I've ever met, but damn, she commands the attention of a room full of people like a drill sergeant.

This whole operation is running like a well-oiled machine.

I don't know how she does it — sees the bigger picture like she does. I guess I do the same thing, but on a much, much smaller scale.

This makes the setup I have look like child's play.

I peer inside one of the boxes I've just put down and it's full of lanterns that need to be hung.

"Bloody lanterns," I mutter under my breath.

"You can go up to bed if you want." I hear her voice right before I feel her arms wrapping around my waist.

"I'm fine," I say as I twist around so I can look at her.

I'm exhausted, but I'd stay here all night if it meant that she'd smile at me the way she is right now.

"No, *seriously*, the team will only work for another hour and then we'll be back into it at a more reasonable hour. Go and get some rest. I'll be up soon."

She hasn't officially moved in yet, all her boxes of crap are still waiting for a moving truck, but she hasn't spent a night out of my bed in over a week and a half — so it's as good as official as far as I'm concerned.

"If you insist."

"I do." She turns me by my shoulders and gives me a shove in the direction of the staircase.

I'm halfway to freedom when I hear my name being called from across the room.

"So close," I mutter to myself.

Gabriel, the owner of the place next door, waves me down and gestures for me to wait for him to come over.

He's got about five hundred string lights, a million lanterns and layer upon layer of something called *tulle* to get through, so I point out the booth in the corner that has somehow managed to come out unscathed thus far.

I slide into a chair and refrain from laying my head down on the table. He's likely been up for as long as I have, so at least maybe that'll help keep this brief.

He sits down opposite me and looks over his shoulder like he's afraid of what might come at him while he's not looking.

"Scary shit, right?" I joke. "Sorry about all the noise."

He waves his hand dismissively. "It's no problem, but you're right, this is terrifying. Since when do you host weddings?"

"Since I decided I wanted to impress a woman," I say with a roll of my eyes.

"Not the bride I hope?"

I chuckle. Gabriel has such a good sense of humour, for a man in his seventies, he's still so young at heart.

"The bridesmaid," I clarify.

"Ahh I see..." He nods his head in understanding. "What happened to that pretty young woman you brought into my place?"

"Same pretty young woman."

His eyes light up. "Oh good. I liked her."

I try and bite back a yawn. "I don't mean to be rude, but what can I do for you at this hour?"

He looks at me sheepishly. "I know it's not a good time, but I wanted to plant the seed now."

I'm not sure where he's heading with this, but I'm intrigued.

"Go on."

"I've decided I'm going to retire at the end of the year. And I want to sell my place to someone I like, someone I trust..."

"And you want to know if I know of anyone?" I ask, confused.

He shakes his head. "No, I want to sell it to *you*."

I laugh, but it dies off quickly when I see his expression.

He's deadly serious.

"I think I might already have my hands full with this place."

"You're young. You can handle it."

This whole situation is so bizarre. There's nothing like doing business at three in the morning.

I go to say something more, but he cuts me off with a wave of his hand. "I just want you to think about it," he says as he gets to his feet. "The offer is there, and there's no hurry to give me an answer."

"Okay?" I say, unsure what else I can give him right now.

My mind is spinning.

"You'll think about it?"

"I'll think about it."

"Excellent." He beams. "I'm off to bed, I'm too old for this nonsense."

"Night, Gab."

I chuckle as I watch him weave his way through the carnage and out the door.

I sit for a few minutes, thinking about what he's just said before getting up and heading up the stairs to bed.

***

I must have drifted off while I waited for her, because I didn't hear her come in, I just feel her cool hands touching my bare skin.

"You work too hard," I mumble as I glance over at the clock by my bedside and see that it's four forty-five in the morning.

"I know," she replies with a yawn as she snuggles in to me. "But we can sleep in a bit later now that I've got some extra done. I don't know what I was thinking, letting her choose a venue that couldn't be set up until the day of the wedding... I need more sleep than this."

"You're doing good, dimples, it's a hell of a lot of work... If I didn't need my restaurant back, you could just leave it set up for another one next week," I joke.

"Oh, don't tempt me. I might never give it back. It looks seriously beautiful down there."

We fall into silence and I feel myself drifting back off again when an idea hits me straight in the face and wakes me up in an instant.

"Holy fuck, let's do it."

"Not tonight, I'm too tired for sex," she replies lazily.

I chuckle. "Not *that*. Let's make a space just for weddings, or parties or whatever the fuck else you want to throw. Let's do it."

She pats my chest sleepily. "You really are sleep deprived. I can't keep your restaurant."

"You're right. You can't."

"You're not making any sense."

She's right, I'm making no sense at all from her point of view, but inside my head, the plan of a lifetime is unfolding.

"Gabriel wants to sell me his place next door," I blurt out the piece of the puzzle that she's missing.

"*What*?" she answers quickly, sounding far more alert than she did only a moment ago.

That piece of information certainly got her attention.

"He came over tonight. He's retiring, and he wants me to buy the place... But I don't need two restaurants..."

"No?" she questions.

I can feel her heart beating against my chest.

"No." I shake my head. "But what I *do* need is a venue that will be perfect for my incredibly talented event planner girlfriend to host weddings and whatever other extravagant events crazy rich people want to throw. Actually, it's not what *I* need, it's what *we* need."

This idea should terrify me after what happened with my last relationship, and the fact that I had to buy Lizzie out of the business and all the other shit that went with it, but I don't feel one ounce of panic about this. Katie isn't like my ex, not even a little bit, and I know I have no reason *not* to do this with her — if it's what she wants.

"Jackson Matthews, are you asking me if I want to go into business with you?"

"I think I might be."

"Are you serious?" she asks, and I can hear the excitement in her voice. "You're not fucking with me?"

I chuckle. "I'm as serious as herpes."

"*Heart attack*, Jackson, the phrase is 'as serious as a heart attack.'"

"Is herpes not serious enough for you?"

"Oh *lord*." She groans. "It's plenty serious; just can we get back to this business conversation already, I haven't had enough sleep to deal with your stupid sayings right now."

I chuckle. "Imagine it, dimples... functions, events... Imagine the possibilities we could create for that place."

"I can picture it already," she admits.

We're lying here in total darkness, I can barely make out the shape of her in the bed, but I've never felt closer to her — to anyone for that matter.

Being with Lizzie felt like work a lot of the time, and while Katie is no stranger to keeping me on my toes; it feels natural when we're together.

"I can picture it too."

"Are you sure you're not just exhausted and losing your mind?"

"I could be. I don't even know what he wants for the place."

"Sleep on it?" she suggests.

I don't need to sleep on it. If she wants it, and we can make the money work, then it's ours, but I nod my head and lean down until my lips find her forehead.

"You need to get some rest."

"You should have thought about that before you offered me the opportunity of a lifetime," she says, her tone teasing.

I chuckle as she snuggles even closer into me.

It's funny, she thinks I'm the one offering her something, when the reality is quite the opposite — *she's* the one with everything to offer *me*.

CHAPTER TWENTY-FOUR

Katie

"Show time, dimples." Jackson grins at me.

I know there's something important I should be doing right now, but I can't take my eyes off him long enough to figure out what it is.

I thought he looked handsome in a shirt and tie, but that's got *nothing* on him in a tux.

The place he brought it from should have hired him on the spot to model the thing for them, that's how good he looks.

Quite frankly, I'm afraid he's going to upstage the groom.

"Don't let him in here," Tillie yells out from somewhere inside Jackson's apartment. "It's bad luck."

I roll my eyes. "It's only bad luck if the groom sees you — not my boyfriend."

"Same difference," she yells back.

He cracks a grin. "I've been instructed to tell you that it's five minutes until start time."

"Well you go back down there and tell him I'll see him in ten, has he not heard of being fashionably late?" Tillie hollers at Jackson.

I can hear the click of a camera every few seconds. The photographer has been here all morning, taking five thousand photos of Tillie's every move. Quite frankly, it's exhausting. My face hurts. I'm used to being behind the scenes, not in front of the camera.

"Roger that," Jackson calls back to her.

"How are you holding up?" he whispers to me.

"I'm great. Now that she's in the dress and has her hair and makeup done, she's starting to calm down."

He raises his brow at me as if to say 'really?'.

"Calm by Tillie's standards," I amend.

He reaches his hand out and runs his thumb gently down the side of my face. "You look incredible."

"Thank you," I say, my tone still hushed. "I'm still not sure purple is really my colour."

He glances down at what I'm wearing. "It's a nice dress, but—"

I interrupt him. "If you're going to say it'll look better on the bedroom floor, I might have to seriously rethink our relationship status."

"I wasn't going to say that," he replies sheepishly.

I raise my brow at him.

"*Alright.*" He chuckles. "I *might* have been going to say that."

I shake my head at him. "You really need to work on your game, dreamboat."

He chuckles and turns to head back down the stairs.

"I think I'm doing alright. I got you, didn't I?"

"You're lucky you're so pretty," I call after him.

"Katie!" I hear Tillie yell. "We need you for more photos!"

I watch Jackson and his cheeky grin disappear from sight before I go back in for another round of killing my jaw.

***

"The happy couple are about to cut the cake, so if you could all turn your attention this way..." the voice on the microphone tells us.

Jackson wraps his arm around my waist and turns us so we can watch Tillie and Reece cut their monstrosity of a wedding cake.

The thing could feed a third-world country for about a week, but this was one of the things that Tillie was not willing to compromise on. Not even a little bit.

Tillie beams up at Reece as they hold the knife together and jointly push the blade through the bottom layer.

I've never seen her look so happy or in love.

She really has found the perfect man for her, and she knew it from the first moment they met.

I sneak a look at Jackson, he's watching them with a smile on his face, and a drink in his hand.

It's his first of the evening and he's assured me that it'll be one of only a small few.

Apparently, his days of drinking himself blind are behind him, and I believe him. He's not the same heartbroken man he was when we slept together for the first time.

He's no longer caught up on his ex and the life they shared.

I don't even know if he's angry about it anymore, I think he's simply just moved on and put it all behind him, and I admire that about him.

Sure, it took probably a few drinking benders too many, but he got there in the end and like he always tells me, I'm a patient woman.

"Is he going to squish cake in her face?" Jackson asks me.

"Not if he wants to live." I smirk.

He shoots me a disappointed look.

"Alright, ladies and gentlemen, that wraps up the formalities for the evening, I've been instructed by the bride to tell you all to 'get loose' and 'shake it' on the dance floor. So, go do that." The MC chuckles through the mic and the room laughs along with him.

"You coming to shake it with me?" I ask Jackson with a grin.

"I've just got to shoot out back and check on Bryn, and then I'll be right there," he promises.

He kisses me on the forehead and disappears through the crowd.

He's disappeared an awful lot since the ceremony finished, and it worries me that something might be wrong, but all the food has been perfect, the bartenders have been impressing us all.

Everything seems to be running perfectly.

"C'mon, girl, you're coming with me!" Tillie cries as she strolls past me, grabbing my arm as she goes.

"I just need to check on something," I tell her, but she shakes her head at me.

"Nope. You are officially off the clock. This day has been perfect, sweetie, and I'm so grateful for your obsessive compulsive planning skills, but now I need you to let your hair down and celebrate with me, because I just got freaking *married*!"

I laugh at her and give up on my attempt of going after Jackson. "Who the hell would have thought?"

She shakes her head. "Not *me*, that's for damn sure."

She takes my hands and tows me out towards the middle of the area I've had set up for dancing.

The live band in the corner has started playing and nearly everyone is up here singing along and dancing.

"I'm married!" Tillie shrieks again. "And he's like *loaded.*"

I laugh. "I'm aware, Tills."

I feel Jackson come up behind me and wrap his arms around my waist.

"Having fun, dimples?"

I smile up at him and nod.

"Can I steal you away for a minute?" he yells to be heard over the music.

I nod and let him lead me from the packed dance floor, across the room and up the stairs that lead to his apartment — *our* apartment after this weekend.

"Where are we going?" I ask once the noise dies down enough that we can finally hear each other speak.

"I just want you to myself for a few minutes."

"You just want to see how this dress looks on the floor, don't you?"

"Something like that."

He looks back at me over his shoulder before turning his key in the lock and pushing the door open.

I'm still watching him, so I don't notice exactly what he's done until I'm nearly in the centre of the living room.

There are string lights *everywhere* — just like downstairs, and a huge bunch of my favourite flowers — pink roses, in a giant crystal vase in the middle of the table. I don't know if they're new, or if I was just too busy with the wedding prep to notice, but he's put frames holding photos of the two of us all around the apartment too.

"What *is* this?"

He steps further into the room and then slowly turns to face me.

He looks like something out of a movie in his black tux and crisp white shirt, his entire frame softly illuminated by the glow of the lights.

"I thought you deserved something just for you."

"Jackson," I breathe in disbelief. I can't believe he did all this for me.

He reaches for an ice bucket I hadn't even seen on the table and pulls out a bottle of champagne.

He pours us each a glass as I wander around the room, softly touching the lights he's hung.

I turn around and he's right there in front of me, holding out a glass for me to take.

"Thank you," I whisper.

He holds his own glass out for me to clink mine against.

"What are we toasting?"

"You," he says simply.

His eyes are trained on mine, and there's an intensity radiating from him that I'm not quite used to feeling.

"You did all this for me?"

"I did."

"But you hate string lights."

"I can safely say I like them even less now."

I glance around, breaking our contact, but I can still feel his eyes on me, boring holes into me.

I take a sip from my glass and moan in appreciation, I'd hate to know what this bottle is worth — this is the best champagne I've ever tasted.

"I wanted to talk to you about going into business..."

I flick my eyes back to him. "I'm in if you are."

The corner of his mouth turns up into a small smile. "Oh, I'm in dimples, I'm all the way in."

I can't explain the vibe in the air between us right now, but it feels a lot like that first time between us — just a magnetism, pulling us together.

"You won't get sick of me... Living and working together?" I ask as he takes the glass from my hand and sets it down on the table along with his own.

He shakes his head as he turns back to me. "No."

That's all he says, and I can't explain why, but he's making me nervous.

One of his hands reaches for my waist and the other snakes around my neck.

I go to him eagerly, my own hands resting on his shoulders.

He leans down ever so slowly until our lips brush together, just one brief contact.

"I want to be your roommate..." he says before he kisses me again. "Your business partner..." Another kiss. "Your best friend..." His voice is husky and filled with promise.

I close my eyes as he brings his lips to mine yet again. "And your husband..."

My lids fly open and I look right into his eyes. "Whaaa... what?"

"You heard me," he says.

I stand there staring at him, totally unmoving for a few beats.

I know what I heard, but I still don't know what he means. I don't know if he's asking what I think he's asking.

He drops his hands from my body and reaches into his pocket.

He pulls out a black satin ring box and my hand flies to my mouth. "Oh my god," I breathe.

He drops to one knee and I hear myself gasp. This is really happening.

"Katie North — *dimples*." He grins. "You are seriously the best thing that ever happened to me."

He reaches out and takes my hand — the one that's not still covering my mouth.

"I haven't stopped thinking about you ever since I woke up and read your first note. I should have known I wasn't going to be able to get over you when I couldn't even throw it away."

"You still have it?" I whisper.

He nods. "I've still got them both. Apparently, I'm senti-mental like that when it comes to you."

I don't know why, but that makes my heart melt.

All that time, I assumed it was still Lizzie who had his heart, but now I know that I owned a piece of him too.

He squeezes my hand again and I look at him, waiting for him to say what I know he's going to say.

"Here I was thinking that Tillie and Reece were crazy for moving so fast, but when I'm with you... I get it. I don't want to wait another minute for you to wear my ring on your finger."

I can't believe this is happening, but he's right. I don't want to wait either. The bond we share — it feels like we've known each other forever. He's my best friend.

"You just don't want to give me time to run off with one of your friends."

He chuckles. "Bryn does seem awfully fond of you."

I laugh and use my free hand to wipe the tears that are rolling down my cheeks.

He opens the ring box and reveals a beautiful, diamond solitaire ring. It's simple and elegant and he couldn't have picked something more perfect if he tried.

"You remember when you asked me if I was put off marriage forever?"

I nod. I remember. He told me he'd know if he met the right person.

"I found the right person, dimples, you were right there under my nose."

I can't even speak as he slides the ring out of the box and holds it up to me as an offering.

"Katie, I promise to love you, even when you can't stand my cheesy pick-up lines a moment longer... I promise to love you *forever*, will you do me the honour of becoming my wife?"

I barely let him finish his speech before I cry the word *yes* and throw myself at him.

He catches me, barely, and we both tumble to the floor in a heap.

I find myself beneath him, with his gorgeous face looking down at me.

I can't believe I get to look at *that* every day for the rest of my life.

"Do you want your ring?" his muffled voice asks against my hair.

I nod eagerly and hold my left hand up for him.

He slides it into place on my finger.

"It's kinda big," he mumbles. "If you don't like it, you can pick something else."

"It's perfect," I reassure him as I stare at the ring on my finger. "Nothing a trip to the jeweller for a re-size won't fix."

"Is it okay?"

I pull my eyes from the shiny diamond and into his stunning blue eyes. "It's the most precious thing I've ever owned, because you gave it to me."

"That's a bit cute," he mutters as he lowers his lips to mine.

He kisses me with so much passion, I want to rip the clothes from his body.

He pulls away with a heavy sigh. "They'll be missing us down there."

Truthfully, I'd forgotten about all the people downstairs, even about my best friend's wedding.

"Oh my god, *Tillie*."

He chuckles as he climbs off me and pulls me up by my hand.

"Don't you dare breathe a word of this to her, if she catches us stealing her thunder, she'll kill us both," I warn him.

He reaches for my hand and slides the ring back off before putting it back in the box.

"I won't say a word," he promises me, "but on one condition..."

"What is it?"

"When we get married, I don't want all of that." He points downwards. "No offence to your profession or anything, but if I have to see another string of lights, I might lose my mind."

He's so sexy when he's frustrated.

"No string lights," I promise. "No fuss. No drama. Just you, me and our friends."

He grins and pulls me in for a hug. "I knew I was marrying you for a reason."

I press up onto my tippy toes and kiss him as my hands reach for the zip on his pants.

"What are you doing?" he whispers against my lips.

"I think you know what I'm doing."

"I thought you wanted to go back down?"

"I'm going down alright," I tell him as I drop to my knees in front of him.

"Oh, sweet Jesus." He groans as I free his hard length.

"I told you I'd make it worth your while." I smirk as I take him into my mouth.

EPILOGUE

Jackson

I'm about halfway through my shift when I hear the words no one in the hospitality industry wants to hear.

"Excuse me, can I talk to you for a moment?"

I look down the bar at the woman who has just spoken to me. She doesn't have your typical 'I need to speak to the manager haircut', but pains in the ass come in all shapes and sizes I guess.

I step down the bar so we're face to face, while my eyes roll internally. "How can I help you this evening?"

"Are you the manager here?"

Technically, Katie is the manager over here at the function centre, but I doubt I'm going to get away from this one on a technicality.

"I'm one of the owners, what seems to be the problem?"

She looks surprised. "Oh, there's no problem."

I frown at her. "Then what can I do for you?"

"Well, to put it bluntly... Has anyone ever pointed out how attractive you are?"

I'm not sure what I was expecting her to say, but it wasn't that she thought I was hot, that's for damn sure.

"I tell him all the time," Katie says as she appears at the bar next to the mystery woman. "He's a total dreamboat, right?" she says, her tone light and teasing.

"He's gorgeous."

"Like a real-life Ken doll. He's even got the muscles to match," Katie carries on. "You should see him with his shirt off."

The woman smiles at her. "That sounds perfect."

My face flames. "Um, excuse me? I'm right here..." I interrupt the two of them. "Perfect for *what*?"

I don't know what's going on here, but it feels suspiciously like being pimped out.

"I'm working on a calendar for next year, a hot-guy kinda thing, you know the type... and I'm on the hunt for men who look like *you*," she tells me.

"Oh, hell yes! He'll do it," Katie replies enthusiastically before I even have a chance to answer.

"Dammit, woman, stop throwing me under the bus. I don't want to play model."

"Oh c'mon..." She pouts at me. "You're so pretty, dreamboat, it'd be a crime *not* to do it."

"I think you'd be a perfect Mr. February," the woman tells me.

I shake my head.

"Ohhhhh, pleeeeease," Katie begs me. She raises a brow at me suggestively. "I'll make it worth your while..."

I have to hold back a groan. The last time she made it worth my while I had absolutely no regrets about my decision.

There's something about a reward blowjob that just makes it so much better than a regular one.

"How'd the two of you meet?" the woman asks Katie, with a twinkle in her eye.

Katie grins wickedly as her eyes flash between me and the stranger.

"We met at the bar right next door... He was heartbroken and drunk." She giggles.

"*The heartbroken bartender,*" the woman says as her eyes meet mine. "God that's got a ring to it... Please don't make me beg."

I think again about Katie making it worth my while and sigh in defeat.

"Mr February..." I wince. "I get to keep my underwear on for this thing, right?"

Katie raises her hands triumphantly and grins at me.

"It's a deal," the woman says.

OTHER TITLES

Love like Yours Series
Rushed – Book 1
Pierced – Book 2
Hunted – Book 3
Chased – Book 4

Rock Games Novels
Paper, Scissors, Rock: Vol. 1
Hide and Seek: Vol. 2

My Heart Duet
My Heart Needs
My Heart Wants

Calendar Boys Novels
Mr. January
Mr. February

ACKNOWLEDGEMENTS

The songs that inspired this book – Be Alright – Dean Lewis and 11 Blocks – Wrabel.

As always, thanks to my team – you all know who you are – I couldn't do it without you!

To my readers, thank you so much for your continued support – I hope you enjoy the rest of the series!

ABOUT THE AUTHOR

NICOLE S. GOODIN is a romance author and mother of two from Taranaki in the North Island of New Zealand.

In mid-2015, she started to write about a group of characters who wouldn't get out of her head. Her first book, Rushed, was published in mid-2016.

Nicole enjoys long walks on the beach, pillow fights and braiding her friends' hair. She dislikes clichés, talking about herself in the third person, and people who don't understand her sense of humour.

Please feel free to contact her either via her website, email, Instagram, Twitter or on her Facebook page, she would love to hear your feedback. If you're feeling really game, you can even sign up for her newsletter.

Visit www.nicolegoodinauthor.com for more information.

UPCOMING TITLES

Calendar Boys Novels

Mr. March
Mr. April
Mr. May
Mr. June
Mr. July
Mr. August
Mr. September
Mr. October
Mr. November
Mr. December